BEST WISHES

BOOK 3

Time After Time

Time After Time

SARAH MLYNOWSKI AND CHRISTINA SOONTORNVAT

Illustrations by Maxine Vee

Scholastic Press

New York

Library of Congress Cataloging-in-Publication Data available

ISBN 978-1-338-62831-9

10 9 8 7 6 5 4 3 2 1   23 24 25 26 27

Printed in Italy   183

First edition, November 2023

Book design by Abby Dening and Elizabeth B. Parisi

For Rose Brock.

Thank you for bringing us together! We love you.

—S.M. & C.S.

✳

* 1 *

The First Friday

Hi Maya,

I'm Lucy. You don't know me—yet. But I'm here to tell you about the most amazing thing that has ever happened to me.

And to you.

I got this mysterious box in the mail, just like you did. I was dazzled by the bracelet inside, just like you probably are right now. And just like you, I got a letter that explained exactly what the bracelet was and how to use it.

I vowed not to make any of the mistakes that other people made with this magical (yes, that's right—*magical*) bracelet.

Things didn't exactly go according to plan.

1

I'm going to try my very best to explain what happened to me with this bracelet. I feel like I owe you that much. And the rest? That's up to you.

Everything started Friday, yesterday (though by the end of my story, simple words like *yesterday* are going to have a whole other meaning).

I woke up ten minutes before my alarm was set to go off and lay in bed listening to the *quiet.* The sunlight coming through the window lit up the shelves on my wall:

Shelf 1: Completed Lego model sets

Shelf 2: Fossils (mostly ammonites and bivalves, but also an *actual* trilobite!)

Shelf 3: Crystals

A place for everything and everything in its place—hold on. Something was off.

I slid out of bed and reached up to the top shelf to adjust my crystal prism . . . just . . . right.

The sunlight hit the prism and scattered tiny rainbows all over my walls.

I smiled.

I loved being at Dad's house.

My parents have been divorced since I was three, so I

don't really remember them together. Now I'm ten. I spend half my nights at Dad's and half at Mom's. I love my mom and my stepdad, Ben, and my adorable half-siblings, Kyle and Kaylee (they're twins). But the twins just learned to walk, and they shove everything into their mouths—including crystals. After a few days of diaper changes and baby slobber all over my belongings, I'm always ready to come back to the peace of Dad's place, where it's just the two of us.

I changed into the outfit I had laid out for myself the night before: my favorite red shirt, jean shorts, and the best part—my brand-new Swoop Max sneakers. The leather was so white that it made my eyeballs sizzle.

Mom hadn't wanted me to get them because she said all-white shoes weren't practical. But once I reminded her that if there is any fifth grader who can keep her shoes sparkling white, it's me, she relented.

I trotted down the steps, straightening the photo frames as I went. There are pictures of me and Dad at my yaa and bpuu's house in Krabi, Thailand, from every summer since I was a baby. I frowned as I passed the photo from three years ago, aka the Summer of the Bowl Cut.

Thank goodness my hair grows fast.

"Dad?" I called, rounding into the kitchen.

3

Dad stood at the counter, blending up his signature peaches-and-cream smoothie—my fave. "My Girl" was playing on Spotify.

"Lulu!" he said with a smile. "Come dance with me—they're playing our song!"

I laughed as he spun me around, and we both sang along.

"Talking 'bout m-y-y-y-y gir-r-l . . ."

As I twirled, my hand bonked the smoothie glass and a glob of bright peach liquid sailed out and landed with a plop . . . on the floor *beside* my shoe.

"Phew! That was close!" I said, reaching for a towel.

"I'll say. You can't get your new shoes dirty on field trip day." Dad grinned. "Excited?"

"Beyond," I said. This was the day I'd been waiting for all year. Our fifth-grade class was going to my favorite place in the city: the Fort Worth Natural History Museum.

"And you'll still let me be your special helper in the Hall of Gems?" I asked Dad, mopping up the spill.

"Of course! Who else knows enough about hexagonal crystal systems to be my assistant?"

Dad is the senior geologist for the museum. Normally, he's too busy working behind a microscope in the geology

lab to lead school tours, but he's making a special exception today since it's my school. And the best part is that he got permission for me to help with the gemstone demo!

"Let's get going," said Dad. "If we leave now, we'll be ten minutes early to school. Grab your lunch. Did you bring your frequent visitor card?"

I nodded and patted my back pocket. "One more punch and that free ice-cream cone from Draum's is all mine." I drained the rest of my smoothie.

When I stay at Mom's, I'm usually gulping down a dry waffle as I run to beat the school bell. But this was Dad's, which meant everything went as smoothly as peaches and cream.

We drove through our neighborhood, past houses already decked out for Halloween and Día de los Muertos. Grinning jack-o'-lanterns hung from the twisty live oak trees and papel picado garlands were strung over windows.

"It's kind of cold this morning—seventy-five degrees," said Dad. "I hope you brought a sweatshirt."

"Dad! That's not even cold. Besides, no way am I covering up my awesome outfit." We pulled into the car line in front of my school. I gave Dad a kiss and hopped out.

"See you in a couple hours at the museum," I said.

Dad smiled. And then he blushed the color of red garnet as he looked past me and did a little wavy thing with his fingers.

Huh? I looked to see who was standing behind me.

Oh, *gag.* Of course.

Dad's girlfriend stood at the school entrance holding the door open and greeting families as they walked little kids inside.

Yes, that's right. My dad's girlfriend is Ms. Brock, my school's librarian.

"Good morning, Lucy," Ms. Brock said as I walked up. And then she saw Dad and she did that cringey little wave thing back. I looked at Dad, who was making a heart sign with his fingertips. Ms. Brock giggled and blushed.

Ugh. I seriously worried I was going to be sick. They thought they were being cute!

It's not that I didn't want Dad to have a girlfriend. After all, it's been seven years since he and Mom split up. Dad had gone on dates before and I'd always been fine with that. But dating the librarian at my school? So awkward. Especially awkward because they met *at school*, when Dad volunteered to sell books at the book fair. And Ms. Brock? I mean, sure, she dressed nice and was kind of pretty. That day she was wearing a striped yellow-and-white sundress and cute silver flats.

But honestly? She was way too strict.

"Lucy?" she called after me as I hurried to class. "Walking feet, please."

Case in point.

I mumbled a "sorry" and slowed down as a couple of third graders blazed past me in a full sprint. I turned to see if Ms. Brock would call them out, but she didn't say a word.

Correction. Ms. Brock was too strict *with me*.

I wasn't going to let anything ruin my day, though. I was off to my favorite place with my very best friend in the whole world.

Olive Moore was waiting for me at the door of Ms. Hoffman's classroom.

I threw my arms around her and we both started jumping up and down. "Today, today, today! Museum day!" we shrieked.

Olive's hair was a mass of curls that went down her back. She tossed her curls over her shoulder as she gave me a salute. "You ready for this, partner?"

"Ready!" I saluted back.

This field trip was the kickoff for our science fair. Every fifth grader would do a project. Olive and I were partnered up, so of course it would be the best one of all. I had already picked out the perfect topic for us.

"All right, class, it's time to line up and head for the buses!" called Ms. Hoffman.

As we walked out to the parking lot, Olive leaned in close. "I heard we're doing a scavenger hunt and a dino dig at the museum. The team who does the best at everything today gets extra points added to their science fair grade."

"Perfect!" I said. "I know that museum better than anyone. We're definitely getting those points."

Gabe Hicks and Martin Richardson, in line ahead of us, snickered. "You can give up on the extra credit now, Loserthorn," said Gabe. They high-fived each other.

"Let me at him!" said Olive, fuming. "He cannot make fun of your name like that!"

My last name is Thai, and it's not exactly common. There are only two Usathorns in the whole United States: me and my dad.

"Let it go," I said to Olive. "He's not worth getting in trouble over. We're just going to have to beat them."

Olive and I climbed onto the school bus and my stomach sank. Ms. Brock sat halfway back, directing kids into this or that seat. I had forgotten that she was chaperoning our field trip along with Ms. Hoffman.

Olive and I started to take an empty seat together, but Ms. Brock pointed us each toward seats that already had kids sitting at the windows.

"But Olive and I are partners," I protested. "Can't we sit together?"

Ms. Brock paused like she might let us, then shook her head. "Please take the seat I gave you, Lucy."

I should have known that would be her answer. I plunked myself down next to Jordana Russo, who took a blueberry yogurt and a plastic spoon out of her bag and started to scoop it into her mouth. I leaned over to talk to Olive, who sat across the aisle from me.

"Notice that Ms. Brock didn't say anything to Jordana about not eating on the bus," I whispered. "If *I* was eating, she'd tell me to stop."

"Oh, come on," said Olive. "She probably didn't see the yogurt. Don't be so hard on Ms. Brock. She's nice."

"To *you*, maybe."

The bus started to rumble. We were on our way!

"So can I talk to you about something?" Olive asked. "For our science fair project, I'm a little worried that—"

"That Gabe and Martin will get first place?" I said. "Because there is no way their project is going to be better than 'Texas in the Triassic.'"

"Um, well," Olive said. "I mean, I do love your idea for using the fossil replicas from the Natural History Museum—"

"Right? My dad said we can even bring a cast of a dinosaur footprint! You think Gabe can beat that?"

"No, I guess not . . ."

"Definitely not!" I rubbed my hands together. "Trust me, we're going to have the best project of all time. So don't worry about a thing."

Olive slid down in her seat. "Great. Cool."

"I'm going to my mom's tonight, so you can come over there tomorrow and we'll get started."

Olive turned and looked out the window. I hummed to myself as we drove along, past the park and the neighborhood with the good phở place, and then crossed the bridge over the Trinity River.

I turned to Jordana. "What are you doing for the science fair?"

She had taken a giant slurp of blueberry yogurt and her mouth was full.

"I'll wait," I said. We bumped along the road, getting closer. Only two minutes away now!

"I'm so excited!" I cheered. I glanced at Olive, but she didn't seem to hear me. I turned back to Jordana. "Isn't this exciting? And you didn't tell me what you're doing for the project!"

"I don't . . . I don't . . ." Jordana said.

"You don't know yet?" I asked as we stopped in front of the museum. "Don't worry, you'll figure it out."

". . . feel well," she finished, and then vomited blue yogurt all over my brand-new white sneakers.

* 2 *

A Mess of a Day

Yes, Maya. You read that right. Jordana threw up all over my sneakers.

My new sneakers.

My white sneakers.

My new white sneakers that were no longer white but were now covered in streaks of purply blue. There were also splashes on my shirt and on my shorts. I am not going to go into too much detail about the grossness of what it looked and felt like, but you should know that however you are imagining the situation, it was worse.

There was screaming, and not just by me.

By the time the bus doors opened, I could barely breathe, the smell was so bad.

"I'm sorry, I'm sorry, I'm sorry," Jordana said as she stumbled off the bus.

"It's fine," I said, even though it was *not* fine. My shoes were ruined, and I smelled disgusting. And what was I supposed to wear all day?

Ms. Brock and Ms. Hoffman were acting calm, as if kids puking on other kids was an everyday occurrence. "Lucy, I'm sorry, but we'll figure something out," said Ms. Hoffman. "Do you have anything to change into?"

"Um, no," I said. Why would I bring backup clothes for a school trip? "Can I call my dad? Maybe he could get me a T-shirt or something from the gift shop."

Ms. Brock bit her lip, then said, "I think that would be too much of a disruption. If this happened to any other kid in the class, we'd have to solve the problem ourselves."

But I wasn't any other kid in the class! Why was she so out to get me?

"I have an idea," Ms. Hoffman said. "I brought my gym bag with me . . ."

And so that was how I ended up wearing a baggy EAGLE HILL ELEMENTARY ROCKS! T-shirt and rolled-up yoga pants to our field trip, while my cute outfit sat at the bottom of a plastic bag in my backpack, covered in yogurt vomit.

After I tried unsuccessfully to scrub my sneakers clean in the bathroom, Olive waved me over to where the other kids were gathered in the museum lobby. Ms. Hoffman and Ms. Brock were handing out sheets of paper and pencils.

"It's time for our scavenger hunt. One sheet per team," said Ms. Hoffman. "Use the museum exhibits on the first floor to help you. When you think you've found the answer, write the exhibit label number next to the question. We'll all meet in the final location. After the scavenger hunt, we'll have our dino dig contest and then we'll finish on the top floor for the gems presentation!"

I couldn't stop smelling myself. Hopefully to everyone else, the stench of blueberry throw-up wasn't as strong as it was for me.

"Ew, you smell like garbage!" shouted Gabe Hicks.

Olive growled at him and pulled me away from the group.

"Ignore him," she said. "Let's focus."

"Right. Focus. Okay, this should be a breeze," I said,

looking down at the paper. "I've been coming to this place since I was a baby."

I read the first question out loud.

"*This scaly giant terrorized Texas during the Cretaceous.* That's easy! It has to be *Mosasaurus*."

Olive flipped her paper over to look at the back. "Are you sure? What about that dinosaur that looks like a T. rex?"

I shook my head. "You mean *Acrocanthosaurus*? Nope. *Mosasaurus* belongs to the Squamata order, which means 'scaly.' And it was a way deadlier predator than Acro."

"Well, you're the museum expert, I guess," Olive said quietly.

"Exactly! Follow me!"

I led the way to the back of the museum, where the *Texas Under the Sea* exhibit was tucked away. We were the only ones there. That was a good sign—it meant we were the only ones on the right track.

I smiled as we stepped into the hall. The exhibit is an imagined scene from when Texas was covered by water. Most kids like the big dinosaur gallery best, with its bones and robotic dinosaur babies popping out of eggs. *Texas Under the Sea* is the oldest exhibit, so there aren't any moving parts or touch screens. Most visitors skip it altogether. It is my favorite place in the whole museum.

"When I was little and had to come with Dad during the week, he'd take me down here and let me play while he worked on his laptop." I pointed to the fabric kelp forest. "I used to take naps right there!"

"Aw, so sweet," Olive said.

Blue light from the overhead projectors rippled over my face and arms. "Look at me—I'm swimming!"

We made our way around the sea fan replicas, through a pod of plaster squid hanging from the ceiling, to where the mosasaur was.

I stopped in my tracks. Ms. Brock stood gazing up at the gigantic swimming reptile.

"What is *she* doing here?" I whispered.

"She's a chaperone!" Olive whispered back.

I frowned and craned my neck to read the exhibit label, hoping Ms. Brock wouldn't see me, but she turned around.

"Oh! Lucy, you need to leave this hall. I probably shouldn't—"

My cheeks burned. *She* couldn't tell *me* where I was allowed to go. This was *my* special place!

"Just writing down the answer real quick," I said, scribbling furiously. Then I grabbed Olive's sleeve. "Got it! Come on, Olive. Let's 'leave this hall' immediately."

"Lucy!" called Ms. Brock.

But I scuttled out of there with Olive before Ms. Brock could tell us to use our "walking feet" or "inside voices." I didn't need someone to tell me how to behave in my own museum.

Olive and I rushed around, getting the next answer and the next. Well, *I* got the answers. Olive was less helpful.

"Lucy, are you sure it's not—"

"I got this, come on!"

Clearly, the questions had been written to confuse the reader. But since I knew the museum so well, I could see through those tricks. In every hall we visited, we were the only kids there so we had to be the first ones to get things right.

"We are going to win!" I said as we rushed to find Ms. Hoffman in the *Native Trees of the North Central Plains* hall. I was feeling so great that I could almost ignore the smell wafting up from my shoes.

Gabe and Martin ran in just after us. Ha! We beat them!

Even if they got all the answers right, we'd get more points since we were first.

But as Ms. Hoffman checked off our paper, her frown grew deeper and deeper. Uh-oh. When she handed it back, I couldn't believe it.

"We got *six* questions wrong?" I cried, my stomach sinking.

Gabe and Martin barely held in their snickering as Ms. Hoffman handed their paper back. They had gotten every question right.

"It's fine," I told Olive through gritted teeth, even though I did *not* feel fine.

"We would have done well if you had listened to me," said Olive. She flattened her lips and crossed her arms.

"Wait. You're mad at me? Anyone could have made those mistakes!"

"No, not anyone," said Olive. "That was a total Lucy move!"

What was *that* supposed to mean?

Once the other kids came in, Ms. Hoffman clapped her hands to get our attention. "All right, on to the mock dino dig! Follow me!"

"Hey, *Lucer*," said Martin, making an L shape with his fingers while Gabe snickered. "I thought your dad worked here. Shouldn't you know stuff about this place?"

I fumed. I would show them.

And I did show them. I showed them how spectacularly I could fail.

"But, Ms. Hoffman, that's not fair," I said, pointing to the replica bones that Gabe and Martin had uncovered at the dino dig. "A pterosaur femur and a woolly mammoth skull would *never* be buried in the same layer of sediment. Whoever set up this dig made serious errors!"

"Lucy . . ."

"We deserve a redo! Also, no one found the *Torosaurus* horn yet, so—"

"Oh, stop," said Olive, throwing her shovel down in frustration.

"What's wrong?" I asked my best friend. "Don't you want to win?"

"You don't get it," she said, rolling her eyes.

"You're not exactly being the best partner," I told her.

"Fine, then maybe we shouldn't be partners on *anything* anymore," she said.

I stared at her in shock.

Ms. Hoffman clapped her hands again. "It's time to head to the Hall of Gems, where we will be given a very special presentation." She looked at me and winked. "And I hear that we may even have a special presenter."

I smiled and tried to ignore Olive, who was glaring at me.

I didn't know what Olive's problem was, but now wasn't the time to get into it.

I was about to have my big moment with Dad.

The Hall of Gems is my second-favorite place in the museum. It's very dark, with special spotlights on the gemstones that make them glow like they're on fire. Everywhere you look there are sparkling rubies, amethysts, geodes, and shards of brightly colored crystals. My classmates let out a long "ooooooh" when we got inside. I couldn't wait until they saw our demo.

Dad was there in the middle of the hall, standing behind a table with a velvet tablecloth and a bunch of different boxes set out on top.

"Welcome, Eagles, to the Hall of Gems," he said with his warm smile. "Before I begin, can I get a volunteer from the audience?"

Everyone's hands shot up, but Dad pointed to me.

"Let's have this young lady, right here," he said.

I smiled and stepped up to the table.

He looked quizzically at my new outfit and raised an eyebrow. "What happened?"

"Long story," I whispered.

He nodded and turned back to the presentation. "Inside these boxes," he told the class, "I have some of our museum's most special gems. The ones that we don't usually let the public see."

The kids all gasped as Dad opened the first box.

"The first one is a rare cat's-eye emerald. All of our gems today start out as simple crystals of basic elements. All it takes to turn them into these gorgeous objects is a little pressure and a lot of time." He nodded at me. "Madam assistant, would you please take this precious gem around so everyone in our audience can get a closer look?"

I nodded and held the box out, showing each of my classmates. I felt very special to be the only kid who got to hold the gems.

I made sure to hold the box as far away from Gabe Hicks as possible.

Then I showed the next specimens: the Grimhurst Amethyst, the Edwardian Crystal, even a shard of amber with a real extinct species of dragonfly trapped inside.

Shivani Bhasin, one of the girls in my class, said, "Mr., uh, Dr. Usathorn, are we going to get to see a *diamond* today?"

"Everyone always asks about diamonds," Dad said. "And yes, we do have one here today. The first diamonds were discovered in India over two thousand years ago."

Dad reached for the last box on the table, a purple box, and opened it. The diamond was the size of a walnut.

"Diamonds have become symbols of marriage. Of promises. Of weddings. The first time one was used was in the fourteen hundreds, actually, when . . ." His eyes locked on Ms. Brock, and he fell silent. Then, very slowly, his face lit up.

". . . when the Archduke of Austria proposed marriage," he continued. Then he nodded to himself. "You know what? I think I'll need an assistant for this part, too . . ."

I stepped forward, but then he added, ". . . Ms. Brock, could you help me, please?"

I froze. Ms. Brock suddenly went as pale as fluorite. She gulped and stepped forward to join Dad at the table.

"This diamond is very, very valuable," he said. "It's not mine to keep or give away. But while beautiful and rare, it cannot compare in beauty or rarity to the person who is standing before me today . . ."

What?

And then it happened.

Dad got down on one knee.

I gasped. Everyone gasped.

"It usually takes a little pressure and a lot of time to figure out what you want in life. But sometimes you have to just seize the moment. Karina Brock, will you make me the happiest man in the world and marry me?"

No. No way. This wasn't happening. This couldn't be happening.

My father was proposing to Ms. Brock?!

Here?!

In front of everyone?!

My eyes filled with tears.

Then I turned around, broke into a run, and sprinted out of the hall.

⁎ 3 ⁎

The Box

I ran down the stairs and out the front door of the museum.

How could my dad do that to me? What was he thinking? He couldn't get married! That meant Ms. Brock would be my stepmom!

My head was spinning as I started walking in the midday heat. What if Ms. Brock rearranged our furniture? What if she didn't let me stay up late on weekends? What if she told me to use my "walking feet" or "inside voice" around the house? What if she hated spicy food and we stopped visiting Thailand because she could only eat plain rice and everything in our lives would be bland? Didn't Dad love our family—our little team of two—as much as I did? We were perfect the way we were!

I kept walking. I wasn't sure where I was going; I just knew I couldn't be near the museum anymore. I didn't want to go back to school, either. I made up my mind to walk to Mom's house. It was about a twenty-minute drive, so I figured it would take me . . . an hour? I wasn't sure, and honestly I didn't care.

I hurried past the Cowgirl Museum and kept going through the empty stockyards. I turned left at the big arena where they had the rodeo. And then I turned left again.

And then—

Where was I?

My stomach fell. Was I lost?

My iPad was in my backpack, but it was useless since I had no Wi-Fi. So I couldn't check a map or call my mom.

I wished I wasn't on such a busy street.

I wished I wasn't wearing new shoes. I had blisters on the backs of my heels.

I kept walking and walking for what felt like hours. I ate the smushed-up cheese sandwich that was in my bag while I walked. And then I walked even more.

And then everything got worse.

I heard a siren behind me.

Yes, Maya. A police siren.

I turned around and saw a blue-and-white police car stop beside me. The officer rolled down her window.

"Lucy Usathorn?" she said, looking me up and down.

Oh my goodness.

Was I going to get arrested?

"Yes?" I asked.

"I'm Officer Paperson. And there are a lot of people looking for you right now," she said, her voice stern.

"There are?" I squeaked.

Was leaving a school trip early against the law?

The police officer in the passenger seat picked up a walkie-talkie. "The missing minor has been located."

I burst into tears. My feet hurt, my chest hurt, and even my head hurt. And I knew I was in trouble. Big trouble.

"What's going on?" Officer Paperson asked.

"I'm having a really bad day," I told her.

The sky darkened and a gust of wind went through my clothes.

"Hmm, that's weird," said Officer Paperson. "Not supposed to rain today. You better hop in so we can take you home before it pours."

I nodded and got in the back seat of the police car, hugging my backpack to my chest.

The police drove me to Mom's house.

I dropped my backpack on the porch as my mom threw her arms around me.

"Lucy!" she cried. "What were you thinking, running away like that? We were so worried. I called the police!"

"I'm sorry," I said.

Mom had baby food on her cheek. Kyle was holding one of her hands and I could hear Kaylee shrieking from somewhere inside.

My stepdad, Ben, appeared in the doorway. "Lucy—thank goodness!" He tried to hug me, but he was holding his electric drill in one hand and a plank of wood in the other. Ben designs sets for the Casa de Arte Musical Theater. That's where he and Mom met. Mom is a playwright.

Officer Paperson cleared her throat. "Young lady," she said to me, "we are very glad you're okay. But you can never run off like that again. Do you understand? You've wasted everyone's valuable time and scared a lot of people."

I hung my head. "I'm so sorry."

"I'm so sorry, too," Mom said, pulling me inside. "We'll talk to her."

"Please do. Someone will follow up tomorrow."

Follow up? Would I have to go down to the station? I felt sick.

"Okay," Mom said. "Thank you."

She closed the door and shook her head at me.

"What's going on, Lucy? Your dad called me and said you ran off!"

"I need to sit down," I said. My legs were rubbery from all the walking.

"Why are you wearing these clothes? And what happened to your sneakers?" Mom asked, seeing the stains.

I kicked my sneakers off and told her the same thing I'd told Dad: "Long story."

Ben reached out for Kyle and swooped a shrieking Kaylee up out of her playpen. "Let me watch them so you two can talk."

Mom and I left him bouncing both babies and went into the kitchen.

"I . . . everything went wrong," I said finally. I moved a stuffed monkey and a board book to sit on a kitchen chair. "Jordana puked on me on the bus. And I messed up the scavenger hunt. And Olive is mad at me for some reason. And Dad—Dad—proposed to Ms. Brock!"

Mom raised her eyebrows. "Wow. I knew that he had fallen pretty hard for her, but I didn't know he was planning on proposing."

"Ugh, but why would he fall for *her*?"

"Karina seems like a very nice person, Lucy."

"She isn't! Dad doesn't realize that she's wrong for him."

For us.

"Maybe you should try to get to know her better . . ."

"I don't want to know her at all!" My voice caught.

Mom sighed and took out her phone to call my dad. "She's here," Mom said into the phone. "The police dropped her off . . . Yes, the police . . . Walking . . . Lost, I think . . . She's fine." She tried to pass me the phone. "Your father wants to talk to you."

I shook my head.

"Lucy—" she scolded.

Kaylee was still shrieking from the other room.

"No," I said. I put my head down on the always-slightly-sticky table. "Not now."

"Can you make sure that everyone at the school knows she's home?" Mom asked Dad. "Thanks." She ended the call. "You should never have left on your own," she told me.

I didn't respond.

"The school is furious," she added. "And do you know how scared I was when your dad called me? You could have been kidnapped! Or run over! I know it was a stressful afternoon, but that's no excuse for such irresponsible behavior."

"I'm sorry," I repeated, my throat clenching up. "I wasn't thinking."

More shrieking from Kaylee. Now Kyle was wailing, too.

"Do you need to check on them?" I asked, my face still on the table. Possibly stuck to the table.

"Ben can handle them," Mom said with a sigh. "Honey— I'm sorry today was hard. But everything will be okay."

Everything would not be okay. My father was getting married again. Ms. Brock was going to move into my house. And who knew if Olive was even speaking to me.

Both babies shrieked even louder, as if they were competing to see who could break my eardrums faster. "Do they have to cry ALL THE TIME?" I snapped.

"Don't take your anger out on them," Mom said. "And you are definitely grounded, by the way. No friends and no screens for the next two weeks, at least."

Perfect. Just perfect.

Eventually, I pulled myself off the table. I went to take a long, hot shower, but of course the bathtub was overflowing with the twins' toys. So first I had to pick up all their water blocks and rubber ducks and pile them on the floor. Then I took my shower.

Back in my room, I put on my pajamas, even though it was only five o'clock.

I figured I'd do my homework. But wait, where was my backpack? Had I left it at the museum in all the mayhem?

Hmm, no. I'd had it with me in the police car.

I went back to the porch.

There it was.

And right beside my backpack was a small package.

A red box, about the size of a toaster, with a pink polka-dot stripe across it. There were stickers all over the box, a stamp, and . . . my name and address.

Lucy Usathorn
408 Mockingbird Ln
Fort Worth, TX 76008

There was no return address.

✳ 4 ✳

Nice to Meet You

Who would have sent me something? My birthday wasn't for months. And it was way too early for Christmas.

Maybe it was from Olive. Maybe she felt bad about our fight and she was trying to make me feel better. Maybe she'd sent me a cupcake. Or new sneakers. I picked up the package, went inside, and headed straight to my room.

My iPad rang from inside my backpack. It was my dad. I saw he had called three times.

Mom's "no screens" rule usually didn't include talking or texting. But I didn't want to talk to Dad yet.

I also had one text from Olive:

I hope you're ok. (But I'm still really mad and don't think I should come over tomorrow.)

Ugh, she was *still* mad? For what? Honestly! I didn't do anything wrong!

I ignored her text for now and decided to open the package.

Inside was a blue notebook, some sort of poem on an old-fashioned piece of paper, and a velvet pouch. I tilted the pouch and poured the contents into my hand.

It was a beautiful beaded bracelet the color of coral.

Oh! Pretty! But who was it from? I read the old-fashioned note that came with it:

Because you're blue,
This bracelet is now for you.
Speak one wish to make it true.
(There are some things it cannot do.)
Keep the box to mail the magic off
When you are through.
Take care and beware.
Hugs and kisses,
And best wishes.

Huh? Speak one wish to make it true? What did that mean?

Next, I opened the notebook. The pages were filled with handwriting. I flipped to the front.

Dear Lucy,

Wait! It was a letter to me? I kept reading.

Please read this whole letter before doing anything! Do not put on the bracelet! Do not make a wish yet!

Got that? Good. Now I can start.

Hi.

I'm Addie Asante. We've never met, but you need to know what happened to me.

The bracelet in this box is magic. And by magic, yes, I mean the hocus-pocus kind. Think fairy tales, but without the messy stardust getting all over your clothes and hair.

Wait, what? A magic bracelet? This had to be a joke. And how did this Addie person know my name?

I sank onto my bed and kept reading. And reading. I read right until my mom called me for dinner. Ben had to go into the theater to install the set for *Into the Woods*, and Mom got busy bathing the twins, so I kept reading while I gobbled down my chicken tenders and salad.

According to Addie, when you put the bracelet on and made a wish, the wish came true.

She said that she had gotten the bracelet from a girl named Becca in New York City. She listed both her and Becca's info at the end so I could text them.

I knew that magic wasn't real, so there had to be some other explanation for all of this.

But . . . why would someone make up something so complicated? And write a whole story about it? Whatever had happened, this Addie person *believed* it was real.

Would it really hurt if I texted Addie and Becca to question them? It wouldn't count as screen time—it was *communication*.

I turned back to my iPad. I had a new text from Dad.

Dad: Please call me. I want to talk to you.

I ignored it and started a new chain. I typed in Becca's and Addie's info. Then I wrote:

Me: Hi. This is Lucy. I got your package . . .

Two seconds later a message from Addie appeared:

Addie: OMG! Hi! I can't believe you got it already! I just brought it to the post office today. I'm not kidding.

Then a text from Becca popped up.

Becca: Hiiiiiiiii! Yay! We're so happy to hear from you. We know this whole magic thing seems impossible, but it's real. ★★★

Me: Kind of hard for me to believe . . .

Addie: I guess you didn't make your wish yet then? Good! Talk to us first!

My iPad started ringing. It was Becca! I debated accepting a call from someone who was possibly playing a super-specific trick on me, but decided *why not* and clicked accept.

Her face popped up on-screen. A second later Addie's popped up, too.

They both smiled at me. At least they were both kids.

Becca was white with curly dark blond hair, and Addie was Black with her hair tied back into two braids.

I quickly put in my earphones.

"Lucy?" Addie asked.

I nodded.

"Are you in fifth grade also?" Becca asked.

"Yes," I said suspiciously.

"Me too," Addie said. "I live in Columbus, Ohio."

"I'm in New York City," Becca said.

"And I'm in Fort Worth, Texas," I told them.

"I know! I sent you the package," Addie reminded me. "Your name and address magically appeared on the box after the bracelet came off my wrist."

"This is so cool," Becca said. "What are you going to wish for, Lucy?"

"I still don't believe this . . . I mean, a magic bracelet? For real?"

"Yes!" Becca said. "When I got the bracelet, I wished that everyone wanted to be my friend. And suddenly *everyone* did. My entire class. My principal. My mom."

"Wow," I said.

"And I wished to no longer be the middle sister," Addie said. "And the next thing I knew, I was in my older sister Sophie's body and my little sister—Camille—was in mine."

"I read about it in your notebook," I told Addie. "Great story, by the way. But that's all this is, right? A story. As in, not real."

"Why would we lie about all of this? And how would we even know about you?" Becca asked.

44

"I don't know. Some strange coincidence? Or maybe you really *wanted* the magic to be real, so it seemed like it was."

Becca thought for a moment and then said, "No. No way. This was really real. When it happens to you, you'll understand. But you might as well try putting on the bracelet and making a wish. If it doesn't work, no harm done, right?"

"I guess," I said.

"But be careful what you wish for," Addie cautioned.

"Just in case," I said.

"Right," Becca said. "So what do you want?"

The words instantly popped out of my mouth.

"I don't want my dad to get remarried," I said.

Maybe that wish was too mean. I didn't want Dad to stay single *forever*. I just didn't want him to propose to Ms. Brock! He could get married eventually. Like when I went to college. Not *now*.

"Are your parents divorced?" Becca asked.

"Yup," I said.

"My parents are divorced, too," she said. "Do you want to wish yours back together? Or that they never got divorced? Did you ever see the movie *The Parent Trap*? You could do a magical version of that!"

"No, no, my mom is already remarried and my stepdad

46

is great," I explained. "And I have two little siblings. So if my parents never got divorced, then they wouldn't have been born. And while they are both messy pains, they are still super cute and I wouldn't want them to never exist. Hmm. Is it wrong to wish my dad's girlfriend didn't exist?"

Addie tilted her head. "Seems kinda wrong."

"Argh, you're right." I frowned. "Maybe I could wish that he hadn't proposed to her *today.*"

"But then what's stopping him from proposing tomorrow?" Addie asked.

"It seemed spur-of-the-moment," I said. "Something about the gems and the museum made him do it, I think. Although if I wish that he hadn't proposed, that wouldn't fix the rest of my day. It wouldn't stop the puke from ruining my sneakers, my best friend from being mad at me, and the whole thing with the police."

"The police?" both of them shrieked.

"Yeah, long story."

I sighed. If only the whole *day* had never happened.

Wait.

That could be my wish.

I could stop today from ever happening. Yes! I would wish to do today over!

That way I could never get puked on, win the scavenger hunt and dino dig, avoid the fight with Olive, and STOP my dad from proposing to Ms. Brock.

And also no police. Or being grounded.

I slipped the bracelet on my wrist. I felt giddy. This was ridiculous! But kind of fun, too.

"I put it on!" I said, showing them.

"Oh!" Addie said. "It changed color again. It was purple for me."

"For me it was turquoise," Becca said.

"Okay," I said. "Here it comes! I'm going to make my wish! Ready?" Addie and Becca nodded. I took a deep breath. "I wish to redo today."

The iPad flickered for a second and I felt a rush of air. But then everything felt normal.

"Oh, wow," Becca said. "A redo!"

"Yup," I said. "So what happens now?"

"I don't know," Becca said. "The magic worked for me right away."

"Well, then it must not be working for me."

"Give it a chance," Becca said. "The magic will happen. Maybe later tonight? Or when you're asleep!"

"Oh yes, maybe when you're asleep!" Addie said.

"You'll wake up and it will be Friday again."

"Sure, maybe," I said, although I didn't believe it.

"And watch out for Eloise!" Addie warned me. "She's a very suspicious blond woman who is desperate to get her hands on the bracelet. She followed me around on roller skates! And totally lied to my face."

I remembered reading about Eloise in Addie's notebook. She sounded horrible.

Addie smiled. "Hopefully she's on her way to Canada looking for the bracelet . . ."

I heard a knock on my door. "Lucy? Are you on a call?" Mom asked.

"I gotta go," I whispered.

"Call us tomorrow!" Addie said, and I logged off.

When I got into bed for the night, I took long deep breaths to stop the spinning thoughts in my head. I could hear the TV in my mom's room, and there was a weird noise outside the window. *Scratch, scratch. Scratch, scratch.* Had the neighbors gotten a cat?

Finally, I closed my eyes and chuckled to myself. A magic bracelet? That made wishes come true?!

Whoever heard of something so ridiculous?

* 5 *

Friday Number Two

Maya, by now you have probably figured out that I am a logical type of person.

Which is why the next morning, I didn't jump straight out of bed thinking, *Ooh, I wonder if my magical bracelet made my wish come true to disrupt the space-time continuum.*

When I opened my eyes, everything seemed normal. There were my shelves, perfectly organized. There was the sunlight coming in through the window. I needed to get up and adjust the prism so the light would—

And that's when it hit me. *I was at Dad's house.*

But I had fallen asleep at Mom's house.

I slid out of bed and went to my vanity table. There was

my outfit from yesterday, all laid out on my chair. Cautiously, I sniffed it. No puke smell.

And then I looked down at my wrist. There it was. The bracelet. Had it gotten a little tighter, or was that my imagination? Was it glowing?

I suddenly felt woozy, like I had stood up too fast.

Was I having some strange dream about the magic?

That had to be it.

I started getting dressed. Then from downstairs I heard: *"Talking 'bout m-y-y-y-y gir-r-l . . ."*

The same song Dad had been listening to yesterday.

I blinked a bunch of times and pinched the skin on my arm. But I was definitely not asleep.

"Dad?" My voice sounded croaky in my throat as I went down the stairs.

"Lulu!" he said with a smile. "Come dance with me—they're playing our song!"

I walked into the kitchen as Dad handed me a tall glass of peaches-and-cream smoothie. I set it down without taking a sip.

He held his hand out and twirled me in a circle, dancing to "My Girl."

"Are you ready for today?" he asked.

"Today?"

Dad laughed. "Very funny, Lucy."

I stumbled and knocked my elbow into my smoothie glass. A big glop of peachy goo fell out of the cup and onto . . .

. . . my dazzling white sneakers.

Okay, remain calm.

None of this could be happening.

Dad rushed to get a towel and help me clean it up. "Oh gosh, Lu, I'm so sorry. Your new shoes! And on your field trip day of all days."

I gulped. *Field trip day?*

Dazed, I blotted at the stain. "It's . . . it's okay, Dad. Don't . . . don't worry about it."

He stared at me. "My Lucy, being okay with getting her new white shoes dirty? Do you have a fever?"

Maybe that was it. I had a fever. I was delirious. That made much more sense and seemed far more likely than the wish I made on a bracelet coming true.

As Dad drove me to school, I could not shake the weird, nauseous, out-of-body feeling. I kept looking out the window and wondering, did I see all this same stuff the day before? Had that same squirrel run up that tree? Had that same man been jogging down the sidewalk? Could it be that this was all some kind of very-well-planned-out joke?

But every time I felt doubtful, like the universe was playing a prank on me, I would look down at my wrist and see the bracelet.

And the day on my dad's phone: Friday, with yesterday's date.

And the man on the radio said it was Friday. So it was definitely Friday.

Maybe I had imagined yesterday? But then where had the bracelet come from?

By the time we pulled up to my school, the buses for our field trip were there.

I said goodbye to my dad and tried to ignore the heart hands he made at Ms. Brock.

Olive was standing by the bus doors, waving at me to hurry.

"Hey! I thought you were sick or something!" she said.

"So you're not mad at me?" I asked.

"Huh?" she asked. "Mad? Why?"

"Um, forget it."

I had to be imagining this. I had to be!

Ms. Brock stood in the aisle, directing kids into their seats. Just like before, she split Olive and me across the aisle from each other. This time, I was too confused to protest.

I turned to Olive. "Does anything about today feel weird to you?"

"Like what?" she asked.

"Like you've already done it?"

"Huh?" she asked. "The field trip, you mean? Last year we went to the zoo."

"No, I mean . . . never mind."

"So about our science fair project," said Olive. "I'm a little worried that . . ."

She continued talking about the project but I wasn't paying attention.

"Lucy?" I heard Olive say. "Lucy, are you even listening to me?"

"What? Yeah, don't worry because 'Texas in the Triassic' is a killer idea, and we'll beat Gabe and Martin easily. I've already done all the research and my dad can give us the fossil replicas, so it'll be great. Trust me, okay?"

I needed to focus. Ugh, it was so hard to think when I was having one giant experience of déjà vu.

Wait a second . . .

Beside me, Jordana took her last bite of blueberry yogurt as the bus screeched to a stop in front of the museum.

Oh no.

The blueberry yogurt.

I had forgotten about the blueberry yogurt!

Jordana's face turned green. And then . . .

Well, you know what happened then.

Vomit, vomit, everywhere.

I couldn't believe it. Yesterday *was* happening again.

The bracelet was real! Magic was real!

I got off the bus. My hands shook as I stood in the museum bathroom stall and changed into Ms. Hoffman's gym clothes and then unsuccessfully tried to clean the blue stains off my shoes.

Back in the lobby, I also unsuccessfully tried to clear my mind to focus on the scavenger hunt, but I couldn't calm down. Olive's mouth was moving, but I had no idea what she was actually saying.

"Lucy," Olive said. "Lucy? I feel like you're really zoned out today."

"I am!" I agreed. "It's just that . . . something weird is happening."

"What is it?"

I thought about telling her, but she would never believe me in a million years. "You wouldn't understand," I said.

"Oh yeah, because *you're* so smart and I'm not?" She stormed off.

And that's how we lost the scavenger hunt. Again.

Olive didn't talk to me during the mock dinosaur dig. I didn't have the energy to deal with her right then. Not when I had space-time continuum issues to deal with.

My brain was all fuzzy right until I entered the Hall of Gems and spotted my dad.

And that's when I snapped out of it.

I had wished for a redo. And somehow, for some inexplicable magical reason, I had gotten my wish.

And I was blowing it. Big-time.

I needed to stop the proposal.

I marched right up to my dad.

"Lucy! What happened?" He looked at my funny oversized outfit and raised his eyebrows.

"Long story," I said. "And not important. But, Dad. Tell me the truth—are you *planning* something?"

He wrinkled his nose and gave me a smile. "Planning something?"

"Yes. Planning something. Are you about to make a big, life-altering decision?"

Dad chuckled. "No. Should I be?"

I searched his face for some sign that he was hiding something from me. But he seemed confused.

So he wasn't planning anything. His proposal had really been spur-of-the-moment. Okay. If that was the case, then what had sparked the decision?

I glanced at the table in front of my dad, with all the boxes on top of it.

The diamond. It had to be.

I knew it was in the purple box.

And I knew exactly what I had to do. I had to hide the diamond! If Dad didn't see it, then he wouldn't think of proposing! Problem solved.

Very quickly, I put my backpack on the velvet tablecloth, unzipped it, and then asked, "Dad, what time is it?"

As he looked down at his watch, I stealthily grabbed the purple box and dropped it inside my bag.

Done! Hidden! Woot! As soon as we were finished with the presentation, I would put it back.

"Almost eleven thirty," my dad said. "We should get started."

"Great," I said. "Good luck!" I grabbed my bag off the table and took a few steps back.

"Welcome, Eagles, to the Hall of Gems," my dad said to everyone with a warm smile. "Before I begin, can I get a volunteer from the audience?"

I raised my hand, and of course, he chose me.

"Inside these boxes," he began, "I have some of our museum's most special gems . . ."

He started with the cat's-eye emerald. "Madam assistant, would you please take this precious gem around so everyone in our audience can get a closer look?"

I nodded back and showed them, just like last time.

Then we did the Grimhurst Amethyst, the Edwardian Crystal, the shard of amber.

And then here came Shivani's question:

"Mr., uh, Dr. Usathorn, are we going to get to see a *diamond* today?"

"Everyone always asks about diamonds," Dad said. "And yes, we do have one here today. The first diamonds were discovered in India over two thousand years ago."

Dad reached for the final box on the table.

But there was no final box on the table.

"Hmm," he said. "Where did that . . . did I forget . . ."

I tried to keep my face as blank as possible. Was there a diamond missing? Hmm . . .

Dad shrugged. "Seems like I forgot to bring out one of the diamonds today. Not sure how I did that, sorry. But what can I tell you about our missing stone?" He looked around the room, and suddenly his eyes landed on Ms. Brock. Very slowly, his face lit up and he smiled at her.

"Diamonds have become a symbol. Of love. Of marriage. You know, my daughter asked me if I was planning any life-changing events today, and I said I wasn't. Because I wasn't. But that gave me an idea. We don't need symbols to make big decisions, or to make something real, now do we?"

Oh no.

It was happening. Again!

Dad got down on one knee.

Everyone gasped.

No. No, no, no.

"It usually takes a little pressure and a lot of time to figure out what you want in life. But sometimes you have to just seize the moment. Karina Brock, will you make me the happiest man in the world and marry me?"

I couldn't believe it.

I spun on my heel and ran out of the Hall of Gems and out of the museum.

This time, I was smart enough to know I couldn't find my way home from downtown Fort Worth. I found a lady sitting with her baby stroller on a bench and used her phone to call Mom.

"Please come get me," I begged. "Dad just proposed to Ms. Brock! At the museum! In front of everyone! I can't go back there. I can't! I won't!"

"Okay, honey, calm down," Mom said. "Our Mommy-and-Me class is finished, and I can come and get you. I have to text your father and call the school."

"Whatever! Just come!" I returned the phone to the nice lady and hid around the corner until I finally saw my mom's car.

The twins were screaming in their car seats in the back, so I didn't have to say much on the ride home. Instead I just felt sad. Defeated.

Against all odds, I had made a wish and it had come true. I had been given a redo on the worst day of my life. But I hadn't changed a thing. My dad had still proposed to Ms. Brock.

I had wasted the wish.

Back at my house, I picked at my sandwich and took out my iPad to text Becca and Addie to tell them what had happened. There were three new texts and two missed FaceTime calls from my dad.

But the entire conversation I'd had with Becca and Addie the day before was gone.

Right. Because yesterday was today. And I hadn't written to them today. Which meant they had no idea who I was yet. I also didn't remember their contact info.

Up in my room, I looked under my bed to find the package with the notebook from Addie and the poem. There was no package. I looked at my wrist. The bracelet was still on, though. How was that possible? How was any of this possible? What was happening?

Would the package still show up on my porch? If it didn't, how would I ever get in touch with Addie and Becca?

I went to the porch and checked. No package. I checked again at two. At three. At four. At four thirty.

When had I first seen the package? It had been around five. When I realized I had left my backpack outside.

I looked over at my backpack, now casually tossed on my bed.

And that's when I remembered.

Oh no.

Oh no, oh no, oh no.

Had I—

No.

Yes.

I peeked inside my backpack, and my heart sank when I saw it. The purple box I had hidden in my backpack.

The diamond. Was inside. My backpack!

I had stolen a diamond from the museum.

* 6 *

Jewel Thief

aybe it was the wrong box. Maybe I had taken an empty box or one with a cheap gem. Like a rock from the beach or something.

I opened the purple box.

The walnut-sized diamond sparkled back at me.

I started to hyperventilate.

I had STOLEN a DIAMOND from the MUSEUM! I dropped the box on my bed like it was a hot potato. Argh! Help! I needed help! I needed to talk to Becca and Addie!

I ran outside at five and—thank goodness, thank goodness, thank goodness—spotted the package on the porch in the same spot it had been the day before.

I raced up to my room and opened it. The pouch was empty. Which made sense, because the bracelet was on my wrist.

But the poem and Addie's notebook were inside. I flipped to the end of Addie's book and found her and Becca's contact info.

I sent a new message.

Me: I'm Lucy and I have the bracelet!

Addie: OMG! Hi! I can't believe you got it already!
I just brought it to the post office today. I'm not
kidding.

Then a text from Becca popped up.

Becca: Hiiiiiiiii! Yay! We're so happy to hear from you. We know this whole magic thing seems impossible, but it's real. ★★★

Me: I know! It's totally real! And I already messed it up! And the police are going to pick me up AGAIN but this time they are going to arrest me for being a diamond thief! What if I go to jail? I don't want to go to jail!!!!!

The iPad rang in my hand.

Becca's and Addie's faces both appeared.

"Deep breaths," Addie said.

"Does this mean you already made your wish?" Becca asked.

"Yes, I'm a fifth grader just like both of you, I met both of you yesterday! We texted and everything, but neither of you remember and I stole a diamond! Look! It's here!" I grabbed the purple box off my bed and opened it so they could see. "See? A diamond!"

"You wished for a diamond?" Becca asked.

"No! I STOLE the diamond! Accidentally!" I put the diamond back in the box and collapsed on my bed.

"What do you mean we met you yesterday?" Addie asked. "I only sent the package today."

"Not yesterday-yesterday, yesterday-today." Argh. This was so hard to explain.

"Deep breaths," Addie repeated. "Try it."

I took a deep breath. Then I tried again. "My father proposed to his girlfriend," I explained, "who is also the librarian at my school, and I don't like her. And my best friend was mad at me. And I ran away from our field trip and the police picked me up. And then I got the bracelet. So I called you both and talked to you, and then I wished to redo the day. And then I woke up this morning and it was Friday . . . again."

"Oh, wow," Becca said.

"So wild," Addie said.

"But I was in such shock today that I didn't do much differently. And I didn't even stop the proposal! I made things worse with the diamond. And now I've wasted my wish! Tomorrow when I wake up it will be Saturday."

"Not necessarily," Becca said. "Did the bracelet come off yet?"

I lifted up my arm and showed it to her. "I didn't take it off, no. Should I?"

"No!" Becca said. "I don't think you can, even if you wanted to. Ooh, it's coral! Pretty. And it looks like it's still glowing?"

"Yeah," I said. "And it's still warm."

"Did the clasp appear yet?" Addie asked.

I turned the bracelet around on my wrist. "There's no clasp." I gently tried to push it up my wrist, but it wouldn't budge. "You're right, I don't think I can take it off."

"That's the thing about the bracelet," Becca said. "It slips on, but the only way to take it off is when the magic is through and a clasp appears."

"So if there's no clasp, then the magic isn't *through*," Addie said. "Which means you might not be done redoing today."

"You might wake up to another repeat day tomorrow!" Becca exclaimed.

My heart leaped. "Oh, I hope so! I really hope so. Then I can do this right."

"What does 'right' mean, though?" Addie asked.

I thought about what I had wanted in my heart of hearts when I made the wish. I thought about how wonderful my

Friday *should* have been compared to how terrible it actually was.

"It means I'm going to make sure I have the perfect day," I said. "The most perfect day ever."

"But there's no such thing as a—" began Becca.

"But that's what I really meant to wish for, right?" I asked. "I wanted a do-over because I had planned this day to be perfect and it was the opposite. So all I have to do is fix it so that everything goes perfectly, and then I'll move on to Saturday!"

It all made perfect sense.

"I'll let you know how it goes tomorrow," I said. "Although, if I get another redo, you won't remember me when I call you."

"Sorry in advance," Becca said.

"But the next day we will," Addie said.

"Yup," I said. "When I have the perfect day."

We hung up. It felt good to have figured things out. Tomorrow, I would make sure there was no fight with Olive. No vomit on my sneakers. No police. No stealing diamonds. I would even win the scavenger hunt.

And obviously the perfect day would include making sure Dad's proposal never happened.

Later that night, I got into bed feeling hopeful.

But then I heard the scratching outside.

What was that, anyway?

I got out of bed and peeked under the blinds out the window.

I shrieked.

There was a person wearing a black baseball hat, a black turtleneck, black jeans, and sunglasses standing right below my window. A blond ponytail poked out of the hat.

"Don't be afraid!" she called out. "I know you have it!"

OMG, this woman knew I had the diamond? Was she from the museum? Was she the police? Was I going to jail forever? "Are you going to arrest me?" I cried.

"What? No. I just . . ." She cleared her throat. "If you give it to me, I won't arrest you."

"Take it!" I said. I hurried to my bed, grabbed the box, opened the window, and threw the box at her. She knelt on the ground where it had landed, picked it up, and opened it.

"This is a diamond," she said, confused.

"Yes," I said.

She placed the box back on my windowsill and shook her head. "I don't want a diamond. I want the bracelet. I know you have *the bracelet*."

The bracelet?

Oh, oh, oh. She wasn't a police officer. She was that woman Addie had warned me about. She was Eloise! And she was lurking outside my window. Was she trying to break in? Why was she wearing sunglasses at night?

I grabbed the diamond off the windowsill and slammed my window shut. "Go away!" I said through the glass. "I know who you are! I've heard about you, Eloise!"

"Those girls already told you about me? That was fast."

"Get out of here now, or I will call the real police! I know Officer Paperson personally!"

"There is no need to call the police—I'm sure we can come to an arrangement that benefits both of us. Financially, maybe?"

"I'm not talking to you," I said. "Go away!"

"Okay, okay, I just wanted to introduce myself. I know you only got the bracelet a few hours ago. You must be overwhelmed. Maybe you just need to take a minute?"

I had an idea. "Yes, I need to think. And sleep. Come back tomorrow, and I promise I'll give it to you!"

A big grin spread over her face. "Great. I'll be back tomorrow!"

I watched Eloise slink away into the shadows. Little did she know that tomorrow probably wasn't coming.

If everything went according to plan, by this time tomorrow (which would really be today—again), my life would be fixed and this bracelet would be long gone.

✳ 7 ✳

Let's Do This

The next morning, I woke up and looked at my ceiling.

The ceiling at Dad's house.

Yesssss!

The magic was still working.

I checked the date on my iPad to confirm.

Friday. It was still Friday, and the bracelet was still on my wrist.

"All right," I whispered to myself. "Let's do this."

I put on my red shirt and shorts again. I thought about not wearing the white sneakers so that they couldn't get messy. But if the only way to get out of this time loop was to truly have the perfect day, then that meant wearing my favorite shoes.

"I will form a protective anti-puke barrier around you," I said to my feet as I went downstairs.

There was Dad, dancing to our song and making me a smoothie. "There's *my girrrrrl*," he sang with a smile. This time, I made sure to set my smoothie away from me before he twirled me.

"Dad, can I talk to you for a minute?" I knew exactly what I needed to tell him.

Dad glanced at his watch. "Okay, but at this point we're only going to be four minutes early to school. Are you okay with that?"

"It's acceptable," I said, then went on. "Dad, you agree that you and I have a really great relationship, right?"

"The best, honey."

"It's been just you and me ever since I was three," I went on. "And don't you agree that in all those years we have been super happy here, the two of us?"

He smiled. "I do agree. We really have been happy."

"Dad, you know I love Mom and Ben and the twins. I love being there with them, but when I come here . . ."

"Lucy, I think I know what you're trying to say."

I exhaled. "You do?"

"Yes, honey." He pulled me into a hug. "I definitely do.

75

When you're here, it's just you and me. Calm. Quiet. I get it. And I love you so much, my very best girl."

"Okay, then!" I said, clapping my hands. I'd done it! "Let's get this day started."

As I walked out the door, I looked down and winked at my white shoes. So far, so perfect.

Everything that morning started off exactly like the other two Fridays. The buses pulled up and we started filing on. Ms. Brock was there in the aisle, directing kids into their seats.

Olive turned to talk to me as we moved down the aisle. "So about our science fair project. I'm a little worried that—"

"Um, can we talk about this later?" I said, trying to count the number of still-empty seats.

Up ahead, I spotted Jordana sitting by the window. I couldn't sit next to her again. But I didn't want Olive to get puked on, either.

"Well, I kind of wanted to talk about it now . . ." Olive went on.

"We'll do 'Texas in the Triassic' for the project, and it'll be great," I said. "Fossil replicas: done. Research: done. Gabe and Martin: losers. Don't worry. I have it all taken care of, okay?"

Olive cleared her throat. "But what if we—"

"Later, okay?" I cut in. Then I turned to the kid behind me. "Oh, hi, Casper. Can you go in front of me? I need to . . . tie my shoe!"

Casper shrugged and switched places with me. I saw Olive scowl at me and then sit down in the aisle seat. Casper sat across the aisle from Olive, beside Jordana.

Whew!

I took the seat in front of Casper, next to Benicio Morales. I tried to turn around and talk to Olive, but it was harder to make conversation in these new positions. It didn't help that she wouldn't make eye contact. She couldn't be mad at me already, could she?

The bus rumbled onto the road, and we were off.

Behind me, I could hear the metallic sound of Jordana peeling back the lid of her yogurt.

I held my breath and said a small, silent apology to Casper.

The bus screeched to a stop in front of the museum.

"Hey, are you okay?" I heard Casper ask Jordana.

"I don't . . . I don't . . ." she mumbled.

And then there was a collective "EWWWW!" as Jordana threw up all over her seatmate. Who was Casper this time. Not me.

"Yes!" I said to Benicio. "It worked!"

"Uh, watch out," said Benicio, pointing behind me.

Too late.

Casper stood up and hurled, sending a spray of vomit into my hair.

"Sorry," he sputtered. "The sight of vomit always makes me . . . vomit."

"EVERYONE OFF THE BUS NOW!" shouted Ms. Hoffman.

In the bathroom, I did my best to rinse out my hair in the sink.

Olive watched me from five feet away. "Sorry that happened to you, Lucy."

"It's going to be okay," I said, toweling off. "My shoes are still spotless, so I think I can still achieve perfect-day status."

"What?" she said, looking confused.

"Um, never mind. Come on, let's go or we'll miss the scavenger hunt!"

In the lobby, when Ms. Hoffman handed out the scavenger hunt sheets, I didn't even look at our paper. I grabbed Olive's hand and pulled her to the Hall of Texas Giants, where the dinosaur exhibit was.

Olive was still reading the first question. *"This scaly giant terrorized Texas during—"*

"*Acrocanthosaurus!* Has to be! And there's the label—number 211. Did you write that down? Good, let's go!" I started to pull her out of the hall.

"Ow, where are we going now?" she complained.

"The *Mammals of the Eastern Forests* diorama," I said. "Armadillo, you will not elude me this time!"

"But we haven't even read the questio—"

"Just trust me!"

We were ready with our completed scavenger hunt sheet before Ms. Hoffman even arrived at the meeting spot.

"Wow, Lucy and Olive! You two are really on the ball."

Oh, it was sweet, sweet justice to see Gabe and Martin sprint in and watch their faces fall. Ms. Hoffman handed back our sheet with all the answers marked correct.

"High five, partner!" I said, holding up my hand.

Olive barely patted my palm. "As if you even needed my help."

I looked at her. How could she be mad at me now? We won!

In the mock dino dig, we found more fossil replicas than before (because I had already figured out where *not* to look).

Things were going well, but I felt a little off. I definitely didn't feel *perfect*. How could I feel perfect when my best friend was obviously getting annoyed at me no matter what I did?

And when my hair was still sort of stiff from Casper's regurgitated oatmeal?

I told myself it was normal to feel a little weird. You know, because of the whole magic-bracelet-time-warp thing. By the time we got to the Hall of Gems, I was sure that I was going to pull this whole thing off.

Dad and I went through the demo. Everything went exactly like it was supposed to go. I slipped the diamond into my pocket this time (and made a very deliberate mental note to take it out afterward). *And* I had learned my lesson and didn't say a word to Dad about planning something. There would be no reason that Dad would have marriage on his mind in any way.

Dad and I finished the demo, and the whole class clapped for us. My heart soared. That was it—the demo was over and no proposal had happened! I just needed to put the diamond back, and then . . .

"Lucy? Karina? I mean, er, Ms. Brock." Dad waved us to come closer. "Can I have a moment with you two?"

Ms. Hoffman paused, and the rest of the class stopped and turned around.

Dad smiled at Ms. Brock, and then he reached out for her hand.

Oh no. No, no, no.

Dad took my hand in his other hand. "This morning, Lucy said that she and I had been living on our own for so long. She's right. It's been too quiet at our house. Too lonely . . ."

"That's not what I meant . . . at all . . ."

Ms. Brock patted Dad's hand. "Daniel, maybe we should talk about this another time?"

Dad smiled. "I know this is a little sudden, but . . ."

I had to do something!

I rolled my eyes back in my head and sank to the floor.

"Lucy!" shouted Dad.

I kept my eyes shut as he elevated my head and patted my cheeks.

I heard footsteps as all my classmates galloped over to us.

"She fainted!" shouted Martin.

"Is she okay?" asked Olive.

"Back up, everyone, please give her some air." That wasn't Dad's voice. It was Ms. Brock's. It was her hands that cradled my head. I felt her brush the hair off my face and take my pulse. I stayed very still.

"Karina," Dad said, "do you think we should call 911?"

"She's breathing and her heart rate is steady," said Ms. Brock, sounding very calm. "Her blood sugar must have just dipped. Look, I think she's coming to."

"Wh-where am I?" I croaked. "Dad? Is that you? I don't feel good. I think you better take me home now."

"That's exactly what I was going to suggest," said Ms. Brock with a smile. She helped me to my feet and held me steady.

Dad put his arm around me, but his gaze was on Ms. Brock. He looked at her like she was the world's greatest hero. Were those tears in his eyes?

"Karina," he began. "Seeing you with Lucy has only reminded me what a special person you are. And that's why I want to ask you . . ."

Something inside me just . . . *snapped.*

"Are you KIDDING ME RIGHT NOW?" I reached into my pocket and pulled out the stupid diamond box and threw it on the floor.

"Lucy?" gasped Dad. "The diamond? What—what are you doing? Are you all right?"

"No! No, I'm not!" I pushed away from him. "I just nearly *died*—"

Gabe piped up beside me. "You fainted for thirty seconds."

"No one asked you, Gabe!" I turned back to Dad. "I collapsed on the floor, and the only person you can see is . . . the only person you *care about* is . . ."

I couldn't get the rest of it out. I turned and sprinted out of the hall.

By now, you know what happened next:

I called my mom to pick me up. I ignored texts from my dad. I reintroduced myself to Becca and Addie. I confronted Eloise and put her off until "tomorrow."

After I shut my window, I lay back down in bed, staring up at my ceiling. Some kids in my situation might feel defeated. They might feel like the universe was playing a cruel trick on them. But not me, Maya. I felt like the universe had given me a challenge.

And if there is anything I'm up for, it's a challenge.

One. Perfect. Day.

How hard could it be?

* 8 *

So Many Fridays

The Never-Ending Friday was probably the hardest challenge I'd ever faced, but if there was one thing I had plenty of, it was time. If something went terribly, it was okay because I always had another chance to get it right the next day. You would think that after a couple (or half a dozen) repeats, I would have perfected everything in the day, down to the last detail.

And you'd be mostly right.

The first requirement was avoiding Jordana's yogurt disaster. There's no way to have a good day if you've gotten puked on. It just sets the wrong tone, you know?

"Hey, Jordana, did you hear that there's a recall on blueberry yogurt?" I asked her on my fourth Friday.

She looked skeptical. "Oh, really?"

"Yeah, it causes, like . . . terrible growths. And rashes. On your face!"

Jordana scooped another giant purple spoonful into her mouth. "Yeah right, Lucy."

The bus pulled into the parking lot of the museum. I heard Jordana make the gross glugging sound in the back of her throat. I reached into my backpack . . .

And this time, when she hurled, I held the giant trash bag out in front of her.

"What?" asked Olive, amazed. "Lucy, how did you have a random trash bag in your backpack?"

I smiled, glancing down at my perfectly clean sneakers. "I just had a feeling it would come in handy."

After that day, I realized that there was no way to get Jordana not to puke (girl loves her yogurt—even if eating it on a bus clearly makes her sick), and I could never convince Ms. Brock to let me sit far away from her (because of course, Ms. Brock couldn't do anything nice for me). So the trash bag solution became my go-to, although it did always make Olive suspicious as to *why* I was carrying a heavy-duty garbage bag in my backpack.

The scavenger hunt was a pretty easy part of the day to

perfect. It got to where I could remember all the exhibit label numbers in order. I could fill out the whole thing before Olive even wrote her name on the top.

Other things took more practice, like the mock dino dig.

"Olive, don't dig so far to the side," I hissed.

"Why not?" she asked, pausing with her shovel in the air.

It was my sixth Friday (or was it the seventh?), and by this time I had determined that the only "fossil" near the edge of the courtyard was one *Protohadros* tibia.

"Just trust me, and let's stick to the center," I said, leading the way to a spot that I hadn't seen any kids digging in yet.

Ms. Brock walked by us and said, "Now, Lucy, don't get discouraged if you don't find all the fossils," she said. "Remember that this isn't a treasure hunt. It's all about appreciating the *paleontological process.*"

I waited until Ms. Brock had sat down next to Ms. Hoffman on a bench before rolling my eyeballs to the sky.

Oh, come on.

The point of this dig was to find stuff, and I was determined to find that elusive *Torosaurus* horn if it took me fifty Fridays.

"You dig right there," I told Olive. "And I'll start here. Don't forget to go pretty deep. You were kind of digging too shallow before."

"You're not supposed to dig deep," said Olive. "What if we damage the fossils?"

"How can you damage a fake plaster fossil with a plastic shovel?"

She put her hands on her hips. "We're not supposed to know that the fossils are fake. This is supposed to be like a real dig. We're supposed to stop and make observations."

I waved my fingers in the air. "Observations take too long! We find the fossil, we win the points. Come on, let's get going or Gabe will beat us again!"

"What do you mean 'again'?" said Olive. "We beat him in the scavenger hunt."

Ugh. Didn't she realize that I was doing this for her, too? If we found that *Torosaurus* horn, then we'd be well on our way to winning the extra credit.

I loved Olive, but sometimes she didn't get it.

We didn't uncover the *Torosaurus* horn that day, but we did find a *Shuvosaurus* skull. Not bad.

As we walked toward the Hall of Gems, I whispered to Olive, "Hey, are you mad at me?"

"No, but . . ."

"Good!" I said quickly. Because if Olive was mad at me, that would make the day not perfect, and that was unacceptable.

But, Maya, no matter what I did, no matter how furiously I dug, no matter how badly I crushed Gabe Hicks in the scavenger hunt, the day always ended up completely ruined.

Because no matter what I did, I could not stop my dad from proposing to Ms. Brock.

*　　*　　*

Actually, I did stop him once, but it was awful (maybe even more awful than the fake fainting). I tried just coming out and telling Dad not to propose to Ms. Brock. I asked to talk to him privately outside the Hall of Gems, and the conversation ended in tears—his *and* mine—and me screaming at the top of my lungs, "I don't want it! I don't want it!" like a toddler who won't put on her shoes.

Not my finest moment, Maya.

And even though he didn't propose (because of my epic meltdown), I still woke up to Friday again. I wasn't surprised. Making myself look like the world's biggest jerk was not part of a perfect day.

No, if I was going to stop the proposal, it had to be natural.

One Friday, I tried locking Ms. Brock in the bathroom.

Turns out she knew this cool credit card trick to get out of a locked room.

"How did you do that?" Olive asked Ms. Brock, amazed.

She laughed and showed us. "I saw it on YouTube," she said.

Another time, I tried setting off the museum fire alarm.

Dad just proposed in the parking lot. He said something about how the danger made him fall in love even more (blech).

The only good thing about the repeat Fridays was getting to know Becca and Addie.

I heard all about Addie's sisters and her best friends and how she wanted to write her own songs. She even sang me one she wrote called "Together." It was really good, and she tried to teach me and Becca the harmonies.

And Becca told us about her brother, and her dad, and how hard it was for her when her dad moved to California.

She told us that her new friend Willow was sleeping over on Saturday night. She also read us the first chapter of a new story she's writing—about a girl who finds out that her mother is a mermaid. It was really good, too.

No matter what we talked about, Addie and Becca never stopped pumping me up to believe that I could make my wish work and get out of this time loop—eventually. Now I had another reason for wanting to break the Forever-Friday. I wanted us to be real friends, friends who remembered one another after the day was over.

And then there was Eloise.

She was always there in her black outfit and sunglasses at night. Sometimes I ignored her. Sometimes I pumped her for information. Sometimes I yelled, "Eloise, go away!"

She was always surprised that I knew her name.

"Oh, I know you all right. And I know you're looking for this." I held up my hand to show her the bracelet. "Is that your spy outfit?"

"It is," she admitted. "I guess it didn't work. But how did you even know I was here?"

"How did *you* know *I* was here?" I asked, on the fifth Friday.

She pointed to her necklace. "This gold bead is a kind of radar. It was originally on the bracelet and can lead me to wherever the bracelet is. It only works when the magic is working. When the bracelet is off, well, the radar is off, too."

"But how did you get here so fast? Wasn't the bracelet just in Ohio a few hours ago?"

"Yup. And the girl there tried to send me to Canada. But I didn't trust her, and I waited by the post office. I saw the street name, city, and state on the box as it went through the sorter, but not the exact address. And then it was just gone. Luckily, I have access to a private plane, so I jumped on it. And once I got to Fort Worth, Texas, the radar kicked in and sent me right to your window."

"Private plane?" I asked.

She nodded and flipped her ponytail like it wasn't a big deal. "I'll take you on it if you give me the bracelet. Where do you want to go? Name a place, anywhere in the world!"

I knew instantly where I'd pick: Krabi, Thailand. It's where my dad was born and where my grandparents still have a house. It's right on the beach, with blue water all around. I wondered if Eloise had room in her private plane for my dad, too. I knew that he loved the ocean and missed it so much.

I shook my head to snap myself out of it. "I'm not getting on a plane with you. Go away!"

I slammed the window shut.

On Friday number seven, I asked her how long she'd had the tracking bead for.

"A while," she said.

"Six months?"

"Longer than that," she said.

"Two years?"

"Longer."

"Six years?"

"About fifteen," she said.

"What? You've been chasing a bracelet around the country for fifteen years?" I asked, incredulous.

"No! I only started doing that two weeks ago, when I felt the pull of the bead in New York City. Before that I just carried the bead around with me. I'd worn it for fifteen years, waiting. And then Becca walked by me, and the radar kicked in . . . and now I'm not letting the bracelet slip away."

"But where did you even get the bead from?"

"Someone I knew got the bracelet when she was a kid. And I tried to . . . you know what? I'm happy to tell you more for a trade."

"What's the trade?"

"Give me the bracelet, and I'll tell you the story."

"Not happening."

"Think about it. It's a great story. I'll even throw in a trip. Anywhere you want to go? I have a private—"

"Plane, I know, I know. Go away, Eloise!" I slammed the window shut. I got back under my covers.

I was getting a bit tired of Eloise. I was getting a bit tired of trying to have the perfect day.

I had tried everything. I had done it all.

I sat up in bed.

Maybe that was it. Maybe I was *doing* too much.

Maybe if I did nothing instead, then the proposal would never happen. And then this day would finally end.

* 9 *

Out of the Equation

The next morning, I stayed in bed until Dad called out, "Honey, are you coming down? Your smoothie is ready!"

I lay still under my covers.

I heard footsteps coming up the stairs, and then Dad knocked on my door and opened it.

"Honey, we're only going to be two minutes early at this rate. Did you oversleep?" he said.

"I can't go," I said, trying to sound congested.

"What? It's the big day!"

"I'm sick. Really sick." I fake coughed. "I've been coughing all night. And I have a terrible headache. And I'm dizzy! I might throw up!"

"Oh no," Dad said, sitting down beside me. "But you've been looking forward to today for so long."

"I know. I can't believe it, either. But it would be very irresponsible of me to go to school and spread germs to everyone on the bus and at the museum, right?"

"Do you have a fever?" he asked. I pulled the covers down and let him feel my forehead. "I suppose you feel a little warm."

I fake coughed again. "I'm a lot warm, I can tell."

I knew Dad would believe me since I'd never asked to miss a day of school in my entire life, never mind asking on my most anticipated day of the year.

He frowned. "Okay, I guess you can stay home. But I

have to go in because they're counting on me to do the Hall of Gems demo."

I had thought about trying to get Dad to stay home with me, but I knew he wouldn't. He had even more perfect attendance than I did.

"Give your mom and Ben a call, and I'm sure you can go over there if you keep your distance from the twins. I'll ask Ms. Muñoz from across the street to be backup until you go." He started toward the door, then turned back to me. "I'm sorry you won't be there to help me, Lulu. You're still my best girl, you know that, right?"

My stomach twisted into tangles, and not just because of my tarnished attendance record. My dad was being so sweet. If only I could freeze time right *now* instead of having it barrel on toward a future I didn't want.

"Thanks, Dad," I said. "I'll be fine. And I'll text you when I get to Mom and Ben's."

I waited until I heard his car pull out of the driveway and then I grabbed my iPad to text Becca and Addie. I hoped that they hadn't left their houses for school yet.

Since our chain was gone, I started a new one. Luckily, by now I knew their info by heart.

Of course I knew they wouldn't remember me, so I had to do the introductions all over again.

Me: Hi! It's Lucy! I got your package and my wish was to do the day over and now I'm stuck in this day!

Becca: Lucy? Who are you?

Me: Addie Asante sent me the package. It had your contact info in it.

Addie: It's me!!!!!!!!!!!!!!! Addie!!!!!!!!!!!!!!!!!!!!!!!! 🏃‍♀️🎈🍦

That didn't sound like Addie.

Becca: That isn't Addie.

Addie: It's Camille! I'm in Addie's body! I get her messages! And I'm so tall! ❤️🤩💅✨

Oh no. It was Friday morning. Which meant Addie's magic was still working. Which meant her little sister was answering her texts.

It was so confusing. My head started to hurt.

Me: Sorry, I didn't mean to confuse you! Addie sent me the bracelet.

Camille/Addie: Addie has on the bracelet! She can't get it off! ✴🐕😊🌼

Becca: I have to leave for school. I'll check in with you both later!

Camille/Addie: I am going to big girl school too! It's the talent show and I am going to be amazing! BYYYYYYYEEEEEE. 👋👋👋👋

And then they were gone.

I stared at my iPad. I would have to wait for Addie to solve her own wish problem, and then I could try texting her and Becca again later this evening.

I spent the morning reading every book I could find on time travel in my room: *A Wrinkle in Time*, the Magic Tree House books. But none of them dealt with being stuck in a forever-repeating day.

At noon, I texted Mom and Ben. Mom was at a Mommy-and-Me class with the twins. Ben offered to come pick me up, but I told him I felt fine to walk over. He and Mom live only two blocks away. Ben had a fried-egg sandwich on raisin toast waiting for me because even though my stepdad is a little all over the place about his set designs, he is on point when it comes to lunch.

For the rest of the afternoon, I tried to stay busy and make the time go by. I knew that if a proposal happened, I'd hear about it immediately.

Two p.m. and no text from Dad.

Three p.m. and no text from Dad.

Oh my gosh, had it worked?

At four p.m., I got a text from Olive.

Olive: I can't believe you missed today!!! Did you know that was going to happen with your dad and Ms. Brock? 💍

My stomach dropped. I felt like crying. It hadn't worked at all.

Me: Yeah, I knew it was coming.
Olive: If you feel better this weekend, come over and we can work on the science fair project. I have a really good idea!

Poor, sweet, innocent Olive, who actually believed the weekend would arrive.

At least she wasn't mad at me.

All of a sudden, my screen started lighting up with texts from Addie and Becca. For a minute, I was confused, but then I realized that they were responding to my texts from this morning.

> **Addie:** Oh! Lucy! I'm back in my own body, and your name is on my package! But how do you have the bracelet already? I haven't sent it yet!
>
> **Becca:** Her name is on the package? But how does she have the bracelet and not the package? I'm so confused! 😕
>
> **Me:** Long story. Wait. You haven't sent it yet?
>
> **Addie:** No! I wanted to check in with you first . . .

I suddenly got sweaty. Oh no. What if because I texted this morning, Addie didn't send the package on time? And then I never got it? Even though I was wearing the bracelet already, what if not getting the package stuck me in this time loop forever and ever, with no hope of ever getting out?

If there was one thing I knew about time travel, it was that one tiny change in the past could mess up the future big-time.

Me: You need to send it to me now! Right now!

Addie: But I thought you had the bracelet already?

Me: I do! But still! And send me the notebook too! Did you write the story yet?

Addie: What story?

Me: Your story! In the notebook! You're supposed to send me the notebook and the bracelet and the poem! So I understand why you're sending it me!

Addie: But you already know why I'm sending it to you!

Me: I know but let's keep everything the same! It's long so you better start now!

Addie: The post office is going to close really soon . . . at six.

I looked at the clock. It was already almost five. Which meant it was almost six in Ohio, because of the one-hour time difference. What would happen if Addie didn't get there in time? I did not want to find out.

Me: Don't worry about writing anything! Put the bracelet and the mysterious poem and the notebook Becca sent you inside and go go go!

Becca: This is so confusing.

Addie: OK, I'm going. Bye! I hope I make it!

I paced my room nervously for the next twenty minutes until I got another text from Addie.

Addie: Made it!

I waited an extra ninety seconds and then I ran to my front door. The package was outside. Phew.

Me: That was close! I'm never texting you all before five ever again!

I sat on my bed and caught my breath. Then I opened the package. Instead of Addie's notebook, there was a red notebook, the pages filled with Becca's loopy handwriting. I opened it to the first page and started reading.

Dear Addie,
I'm not sure I should be writing this. But it feels like the right thing to do. Even if I don't know much about you besides your name...

I read Becca's whole story that night.

And wow, Georgette was the worst. I was glad Becca had Willow—and us!—now.

Before I got into bed, I had a text come in from Dad.

Dad: Hey Lucy, can you call me back? I have something important I need to talk to you about. It's about me and Ms. Brock.

I turned the iPad off. Thanks a lot, Dad. Well, at least now I knew that sitting at home doing nothing wasn't an acceptable solution to my proposal problem.

A problem I didn't know how to fix.

That night, I tossed and turned and tossed and turned until I heard the scratching outside my window.

Eloise.

I grabbed my water bottle off my desk. I leaned out my window. I poured.

"Go away, Eloise!" I called out. "You are evil!"

She yelped. "I'm not evil! Sure, I have some flaws, who doesn't, no one's perfect—but I'm not evil, I swear!"

I shut the window and lay down in bed.

Then I sat up. Wait a second.

Perfect.

I had spent so much energy trying to have the perfect day, but perfect was the problem. The way that Dad looked at Ms. Brock each Friday was as if she were perfect. He was never going to not propose to her as long as he felt that way about her.

I had to get him to see that Ms. Brock was flawed, messy, and totally wrong for him.

The Never-Ending Friday challenge had just gotten a new name:

Operation Mess Up Ms. Brock.

✳ 10 ✳

Imperfect

I knew exactly how to start the new plan.

On the bus, before Ms. Brock directed Olive and me into our seats, I said, "Ms. Brock, could you and I sit near each other?"

She blinked. "You . . . you want to sit by me?"

I nodded and smiled as innocently as possible. "We could sit here, across the aisle from each other. I want to get to know you a little better."

"Well . . . all right," she said, sitting down as I took the seat next to Jordana.

Olive mouthed *huh?* as she took the seat in front of me.

Ms. Brock smoothed down the folds of her skirt. She looked a little nervous. Maybe I had caught her off guard and she was trying to think of some way to be mean to me. "Lucy, I'm so glad that you—"

"Um, hold on a minute," I said, moments before the driver shut the bus doors. "Could you switch seats with me? I get carsick unless I ride on the left side of a vehicle."

"Oh, sure," Ms. Brock said, and we switched so that she sat next to Jordana. "Your dad tells me that the two of you take a road trip every year down to Port Aransas. That sounds like so much fun."

Yup, and we're going to keep taking that trip just the two of us, if Jordana's digestive system cooperates.

At first Jordana hesitated. I worried she wouldn't eat the yogurt beside a teacher. But then her hunger got the best of her. She opened it! She took a spoonful! She took another spoonful! Mmmmm, warm yogurt! She ate the whole thing.

And then guess what happened next.

Yes, Maya.

Jordana's stomach started to rumble. And then she threw up all over Ms. Brock. Her striped yellow-and-white sundress. Her fancy silver flats. It even got in her hair! She got it worse than I did in all my many, many Fridays.

It was disgusting. It was amazing.

I was hoping Ms. Brock would just give up and go straight home, but she was tougher than I thought.

She changed into Ms. Hoffman's extra gym clothes and rejoined our group in the lobby.

She kept on her not-quite-scrubbed-clean silver flats.

She looked ridiculous—and smelled like puke. There was no way my dad would be inspired to propose to her now.

But my work wasn't done.

I needed Dad to not only think she was unattractive on the outside. I needed him to think she was unattractive on the inside.

I had a plan for that, too.

After Olive and I raced through the scavenger hunt, I saw Ms. Brock set down her school lanyard that had her car keys attached. When she turned around, I took them.

I know that sounds bad, but I wasn't going to steal her car or anything. I just needed her to be flustered. I went directly to the museum's Lost and Found and dropped the keys off there before anyone could see me.

It worked. Ms. Brock searched for her keys everywhere, getting more and more frustrated. When she finally found them at the Lost and Found, she came back super grumpy.

Then, to make her even grumpier, during the dino dig, I made sure that Olive and I were positioned right behind the only bench in the entire courtyard.

"Why are you scooping up so much dirt in your shovel?" asked Olive.

"Oh, am I?" I said, glancing over my shoulder to make sure Ms. Brock was still coming this way. "Hadn't noticed."

I flung the dirt over my shoulder just as Ms. Brock sat down on the bench. She shrieked as the sandy dirt hit her in the back of her head.

"Oh my gosh, Ms. Brock, I didn't see you!" I cried dramatically. "I'm so sorry. I was just *so* into the paleontological process that I guess I got carried away."

"It's fine," she said, brushing the dirt off herself. "Do I have anything on my face?"

She wiped her face with the back of her hand, smearing a big streak of brown onto her cheek.

"Nope, you look great!"

I know that sounds harsh, too. But I told myself it was all for the best.

By the time we got to the Hall of Gems, not only did Ms. Brock smell horrible, her face was covered in dirt, her arms were crossed, and her jaw and fists were clenched. Nothing about her was screaming, *Propose to me, I'm very lovable!*

"Can I go to the bathroom?" Debbi Wang asked.

"No!" Ms. Brock snapped. "Stay here! Let's just get this done, and you'll go to the bathroom later."

Yup.

She'd had enough and wanted to go home.

And that's when my dad walked in.

"New shirt?" my dad asked, smiling at Ms. Brock.

"I don't even know where to start," she said, keeping her eyes to the ground. "It's been quite a day."

"I'm sorry," he said, putting his arm around her. Did he not notice the smell? How was that possible? She smelled truly disgusting!

"Don't get too close," she said, avoiding eye contact with him. "I must smell terrible."

"Doesn't bother me," he said.

"Please," she said. "I'm a wreck. I can't wait to get home and pretend this whole day didn't happen."

Relatable.

"You look adorable," Dad said.

His eyes got that googly look again.

No, no, no.

"Karina, what if I can turn this day around?"

No, no, noooooo.

"I don't think you can," she said.

"Karina. I love you so much."

OMG, no. Dad, come on!

"Would you marry me?"

Argh! Still! How was that possible? I give up, I give up, I give up! If he wanted to marry her so badly, FINE. I couldn't stop it!

And that's when I heard her response.

"No."

Wait, *what*?

"Daniel, I can't . . ." she said quietly.

"But, Karina . . ." Dad started to say.

"I just want to go home," she said. And that's when she turned around and ran out of the room, leaving all of us shocked and staring after her.

* 11 *

Checkmate

I couldn't believe it. Ms. Brock had said no. No!

Which meant . . . I won!

Woot!

I had spent so many days trying to stop my dad from proposing to Ms. Brock, it had never occurred to me to get *her* to say no instead!

I had put her in such a bad mood that she had turned my dad down!

Plus? I did not have puke on my shoes, Olive was not mad at me, and we had won the scavenger hunt.

Which meant that this Forever-Friday was over. Tomorrow I would wake up at my mom's and it would be Saturday.

Yes!

I hurried up to my dad and patted him on the arm. "Sorry about that, Dad. But she doesn't deserve you. Are you okay?"

"I'll . . . be okay," he said carefully.

"Let's go home," I said.

I offered to stay at my dad's that night, but he said he'd be all right.

And he would. He would find someone much better than Ms. Brock . . . in a few years. There was no rush.

Once the package arrived at Mom's house, I opened it and called Addie and Becca on FaceTime.

"Hi!" I squealed. "It's me, Lucy. You sent me the bracelet!"

Addie's jaw dropped. "I just sent it!"

"I know!" I said. "And I already made my wish." I ran through a recap of everything as quickly as I could. "I got exactly what I needed, and everything is great."

"Wow, that was fast," said Becca.

I chuckled to myself because actually it had taken *forever* to get to this moment of glory. "Everything is perfect now," I said with a happy sigh.

"So the bracelet came off already?" Becca asked.

Uh-oh. I looked down at my arm. "No, not yet."

"Did the clasp appear?" Addie asked. "It should have as soon as everything worked out. At least, that's what happened with both of us."

"Maybe the clasp will appear at the stroke of midnight?" I asked. Getting Ms. Brock to say no to the proposal was the key to everything. It had to be.

"Maybe," Becca said, but she looked doubtful.

"Good luck," said Addie. "Call us in the morning and let us know."

I got off the call and stared at my ceiling. It would work. It had to.

I vowed to stay awake until the clasp appeared so I could make this day end once and for all. But I must have fallen asleep, because the next thing I knew, morning sunshine was streaming through the windows.

Ah, Saturday. Finally!

Never had I been so happy for a Saturday to arrive.

I rolled over with a big yawn and stretched out in a sunbeam. My alarm clock started beeping and I reached out to turn it off.

Wait.

Why was my alarm clock going off on a Saturday?

And that's when I looked at my wrist and saw it. The bracelet was still there. No clasp to be seen.

I was still at my dad's house.

It was still Friday.

I pounded my fist against my mattress. Was I stuck in this time loop forever?

* 12 *

Detective Work

I didn't understand.

I had done everything right! I had avoided the puke, I had won the scavenger hunt contest, and most importantly, I had stopped the engagement.

"Lucy?" Dad's voice called out from downstairs. "Honey, you don't want to be late for your field trip!"

I got dressed and then paced up and down in my bedroom. I had to think. How could this have happened?

Dad appeared in my doorway, peach smoothie in hand. "You better drink this fast, or we're only going to be four minutes early for school."

"Uh, yeah, okay, I'm coming."

I took the smoothie and then followed him downstairs. Something had gone wrong—but what?

As I got onto the bus, I watched Ms. Brock directing kids into their seats. For the first time, I noticed that she seemed preoccupied. Like she was thinking about something that was stressing her out. What could she be nervous about?

I sat down across the aisle from Olive, as always. My best friend once again started saying that she was worried about our science fair project.

"Lucy, are you listening to me?" Olive asked. "You have a funny look on your face."

"Hmm? Oh yes, the science fair," I said. "Don't worry, and leave everything to me. We're all set, okay?" I craned my neck to get a better look at Ms. Brock. "Have you ever had the feeling that you got something really wrong?"

Olive snorted. "First time for everything, I guess."

"What do you mean?"

Olive shrugged. "I've never heard *you* admit to getting anything wrong, that's all."

I was about to ask her what she meant by that when Jordana started eating her yogurt and I had to go into anti-puke battle mode with the garbage bag, which took up all my focus.

I went through the rest of the day in a kind of daze, trying to figure out where I had messed up.

It wasn't until we got to the Hall of Gems and I saw my dad, standing behind the demonstration table, that it hit me.

So far, I hadn't done anything to mess up the proposal or Ms. Brock. She didn't smell like puke, and she didn't have dirt all over her face. And yet, just like the day before, she would not make eye contact with Dad. It was like she was dreading what he was about to say.

Oh my gosh.

I had always run out of the room when he proposed to Ms. Brock. In every single day that repeated, I had never stayed to hear how the whole thing went. Except for yesterday, when Ms. Brock had said no. But on all the other days, I never wanted to watch her accept (ew) and kiss Dad (double ew).

Shivani asked, "Mr., uh, Dr. Usathorn, are we going to get to see a *diamond* today?"

"Everyone always asks about diamonds," Dad said, like always. "And yes, we do have one here today . . . Diamonds have become symbols of marriage. Of promises. Of weddings. The first time one was used was in the fourteen

121

hundreds, actually, when . . ." His eyes locked on Ms. Brock, and he fell silent. He smiled at her.

". . . when the Archduke of Austria proposed marriage," he continued. Then he nodded to himself.

Ms. Brock kept her eyes on the floor. She looked like she wanted to be anywhere else but here.

". . . Ms. Brock, will you help me and be my second assistant?" Dad asked.

"Oh, um, sure," she said, biting her lip.

I planted my feet firmly on the floor.

This time, I was going to stay and see what happened next.

Dad went down on one knee.

"This diamond is very, very valuable," he said. "It's not mine to keep or give away. But while beautiful and rare, it cannot compare in beauty or rarity to the person who is standing before me today . . . Karina Brock, will you make me the happiest man in the world and marry me?"

I took a deep breath and fought the urge to bolt.

Ms. Brock looked at my dad. She closed her eyes.

And whispered, "I'm sorry. I . . . just can't."

The whole class stared in shocked silence as Ms. Brock

backed away from my dad and then turned and ran out of the room.

I couldn't believe it. She said *no*. After all that work I had done to mess up the proposal, she didn't even accept it! Maybe she was *never* going to accept!

Ms. Hoffman said awkwardly, "Uh, well, now, fifth grade, let's all line up near the door, and, um, let's thank Dr. Usathorn for his very nice presentation."

The class clapped softly. Dad looked like he wanted to sink into the center of the earth.

"Dad . . ." I said, but he took a few steps back from me.

"I, um, I have to go turn in some paperwork real quick, okay?" he said to me. "If you just wait at the front desk, I'll meet you there. Just . . . give me a few minutes."

He walked away.

Ms. Hoffman put her hand on my shoulder. "Lucy, are you still planning on riding the bus back with us? Or did you want to go home with your dad?"

"I'll wait for my dad, thank you, Ms. Hoffman."

She shook her head. "Poor guy. I hope that he'll be okay."

"Oh, I'm sure he'll be fine," I said. "Probably just needs a few hours to get over it."

What did this all mean? Dad and Ms. Brock were not engaged. That's what I had wanted all along. The day had been pretty much perfect. So my wish had come true, right?

So then why didn't I feel amazing?

I looked down at my wrist. Why hadn't a clasp appeared on my bracelet?

Back at Dad's house, I made us a late lunch. His favorite meal—instant Thai noodles with added goodies: imitation crab, green onions, and chopped-up chilies. He sat at the kitchen table, looking terrible. I guess it's not every day that

you propose to your girlfriend in front of a crowd of fifth graders who witness you getting rejected.

"Lucy's house specialty, coming up!" I said cheerfully as I presented the dish to him at the dining table.

He poked at it. "Karina loves Thai noodles," he said with a sigh.

I snorted. "She probably has to eat it mild, with cheese sprinkled on top."

"Oh no, she loves spicy food." Dad gave a little chuckle. "She can eat spicier than me. She loves trying new things, and going to new places. She's never been to Thailand before, but I wanted to take her there on our . . . on our . . ."

Oh gosh, I had to change the subject before he started talking about the honeymoon that was never going to happen!

"Dad, maybe we could get a dog or something . . ."

But Dad was determined to be sad.

He sighed. "You know what I love the most about her? How much she likes you."

My body tensed. "What! She definitely does not."

"Of course she does. Lucy, she talks about how great you are all the time. How you're so creative and bright and how you never back down from a problem."

I rolled my eyes. "All teachers say stuff like that. And if she supposedly likes me so much, why is she always scolding me? She's way harder on me than the other kids."

"I don't know," said Dad. "I'm sure it's hard for her to find a balance since she's my—" Dad cleared his throat. "Since she *was* my girlfriend. But I know she really likes you. She said she was a lot like you when she was young. She knows you can be so hard on yourself, trying to be the perfect kid, but you're already perfect just the way you are." He looked up at me. "When she told me that, I felt like she really saw you for *you*."

I swallowed and for a second I didn't know what to say.

"But, Dad, even if she does like me, things would have been so different with her around," I said. "She wouldn't get our cheesy jokes or our goofy dances!"

"Oh, she's very goofy," he said with a sigh. "She probably doesn't act like that at school around you all, but she's so funny and fun. And her smile." He sighed again. "What a smile."

"I guess you . . . loved her?" I asked.

"Oh yes," he said, stirring his soup. "And I thought she loved me, too."

"Dad, I know it hurts, but you're going to feel better soon," I said. "Right?"

He smiled faintly and squeezed my hand. "Yeah. Sure, honey." The smile quickly vanished, and he hung his head, still poking at his soup without eating it.

I had to get out of there. I couldn't stand seeing him so sad. I didn't want to go up to my room alone, either. I needed to talk to someone.

I thought about calling Becca and Addie to tell them about everything that had happened, but it was too early and besides, I didn't have the energy to explain.

"Hey, Dad, is it okay if I walk over to Olive's house?"

I asked. "She'll be home by now. I'll go straight to Mom's after."

"Huh?" said Dad, barely looking up. "Oh. Sure. Just text me when you get to Mom's."

I hung up my apron, grabbed my sweater, and headed out the door.

✳ 13 ✳

A Sour Olive

"I don't know why he's so sad. It's not like Ms. Brock is perfect, you know?" I was sitting in Olive's backyard on the swing under her big, old pecan tree. This was where we always sat, ate spicy Takis, and chatted. Today, I was the one chatting. Okay, more like talking a mile a minute between bites of fiery corn chips.

"I'm fine with Dad meeting someone eventually, but I just feel like she's not good enough for him. Everything is really great right now and adding Ms. Brock would ruin it! What he really needs is—"

"Stop," Olive said suddenly. She turned to face me.

"Huh?"

"Stop! Can't you hear yourself?" She took the Takis bag away from me and stood up. "You are so controlling! And you think you're always right! You even think you know what your dad needs better than he does."

I stared at her. Olive never used to speak to me like this. Before today—before the Never-Ending Fridays—she'd never yelled at me. Ever.

"That's because . . . because . . . I just do!" I said.

"No, you don't. And what's with the wanting things to be perfect? There's no such thing as perfect. You need to stop it."

"What's your problem, Olive?"

"My problem? My problem is that you don't listen to anyone else. Ever."

"That's not true! Today, I was—"

"See? You're doing it right now! Just like how you didn't want to listen to me when I said I was worried that 'Texas in the Triassic' is too close to what we did last year for the science fair."

"What?" I cried. "But last year we did 'Texas in the Pleistocene' . . ."

"Lucy, I think we should do the Science of Spying instead," Olive said firmly.

"The Science of Spying?" I repeated. "Ooh. I guess that does sound pretty cool . . ."

"It's super cool," Olive said. "We could do something about invisible ink and breaking codes. But you didn't even consider that I might have good ideas. You're not always right, you know. And to be honest? I think Ms. Brock is great. And I think your dad—and you—would be lucky to have her!"

My face burned. "Oh, please. I think that—"

"I know what you think! We all know what you think! You tell us what you think all the time! But you don't care what anyone else thinks!" She stood up. "And now *I* think I need some time alone. See you tomorrow."

And with that, she stood up and walked inside, leaving me alone on the swing.

OMG. I couldn't believe it. I came to my best friend's house to get some sympathy for my awful situation, and instead *I* was the one who got yelled at? Argh.

I sulked all the way to Mom's house, furious. Furious at Olive, furious at Ms. Brock and my dad, but most of all furious at the stupid bracelet. I tried to pull it off my wrist, but it wouldn't budge.

Suddenly, I was furious with Becca and Addie, too. This was all their fault! I grabbed the package off the porch, stormed upstairs, and threw it on my bed.

I called Becca and Addie on FaceTime.

"I am mad at both of you," I said when their faces popped up.

"Um, hello?" Becca asked. "Who are you?"

"I'm Lucy! Remember me? The person whose life you ruined?"

"Lucy," Addie repeated. "As in the Lucy I just sent a package to?"

"Yes! That Lucy! Thanks for NOTHING."

"I don't understand," Becca said. "What did I miss?"

"Lucy's name was on the package," Addie said. "So I sent her the bracelet along with my story. And now she seems mad at us."

"I am mad at you!" I told them.

"Did you make a wish already?" Becca asked. "Did something happen?"

"Yes, something happened!" Argh. I didn't feel like explaining it again. And again. And again. "You should never have sent it to me! Did I ask you to send it to me? No, I did not! And now I'm stuck in this time loop, and I just want it to be Saturday already. I don't even care what happens today! I just want it over!"

"I'm still confused," Becca said.

I slammed my fist on my mattress. "You should have given the bracelet to Eloise when she asked for it! Then I wouldn't be dealing with this right now."

"Eloise? No way. That woman is up to no good," Becca said.

"Didn't you read my letter?" Addie asked.

"Yes, I read it! A million days ago! I read Becca's, too! And so what if Eloise is up to no good? This terrible bracelet is nothing but a curse!"

I ended the FaceTime.

I had to get rid of this bracelet no matter what.

That night, right before ten, I tiptoed out my front door and sat beneath my window.

"Hey, Eloise," I said as I saw her approach.

She jumped back a little. "How did you know—"

"Let's cut to the chase. I know you want this." I held up my wrist and then held up a pair of scissors in the other hand. "And believe me, I want you to have it. You don't even need to take me anywhere in a private plane or give me money. I just need you to help me get it off."

Eloise's eyes lit up hungrily. She started to take the scissors, then shook her head.

"I tried that with Becca in New York and it didn't work."

"I know! So try harder!"

I held out my wrist to her and she pulled. And yanked. I even ran inside and covered my hand in Crisco, and we tried again.

But nothing worked.

"Don't worry," she said, her voice sugar sweet. "You'll figure out how to get it off. And when you do, promise that you'll give it to me, okay? How about I come back tomorrow?"

That word. Tomorrow.

My eyes filled with tears. Before Eloise could say more, I ran inside and locked the door behind me.

I got into bed and stared up at the ceiling. Somehow, today had been even worse than that very first Friday. Sure, the police hadn't shown up, but my best friend hated me. My dad was the saddest man on earth. And I had even yelled at two girls who I thought of as my friends—but who didn't even know who I was. What was wrong with me?

Olive had said I didn't listen to anyone. That I didn't care what anyone else thought. That wasn't true. It's just that I was usually the one who was right!

Except if that was the case, then how come I kept messing up and repeating this day over and over again? Something had to change. But what?

That night, I drifted off to sleep with the word *tomorrow* playing on repeat in my mind.

Would I ever get to see a tomorrow again?

* 14 *

A Brand-New Day

I woke up way before my alarm, before the sun even came up.

The bracelet was still on my wrist, which didn't surprise me at all. I was at Dad's house. Again, no surprise there. I stayed in bed until I heard my dad go downstairs, and then I made myself get up and get dressed.

In the kitchen, Dad was humming along to our song and swaying as he made the peach smoothie. He looked so happy. It was such a total difference from how sad he had been the night before.

"There's *my girrrrrrl*," he said with a smile, sweeping me into a twirl.

We swayed to the song. I tried to imagine what it would

be like if Ms. Brock were here, too. I frowned. Would Dad be twirling her around the kitchen instead of me? What if she hated peaches-and-cream smoothies? Would he start making her favorite smoothie instead of mine?

"You seem really happy this morning," I mumbled.

"Of course I'm happy. I'm dancing with my best girl."

"I won't always be your best girl," I said with a sigh.

"What? Of course you will!"

I scrunched my nose up to keep from crying. "One day maybe you'll meet someone you love more than me . . ."

"Lucy." Dad stopped dancing and held my face in his hands. "Honey, no matter what, even when you grow up, even if you get married and you turn into a wrinkled old lady and I turn into an even wrinklier old man, you'll always be my best girl. You'll always be the most important person in my whole world."

I looked up at Dad's face, and from the way he was smiling, I knew he was telling the truth.

And then I thought about all the nights that I went to Mom's house. Before he met Ms. Brock, what did Dad even do on those nights? He was all alone while me and Mom and Ben and the twins were together. It had been that way for years.

What was worse—having to change smoothie flavors or never getting to be with someone you loved?

It hit me then. Olive was right. I hadn't been listening to anyone else. I'd just been thinking about myself.

I remembered how devastated Dad had been yesterday. The thought of him repeating that heartbreak again and again made my eyes tear up. If I had a chance to do-over my wish with this magic bracelet, I would wish to never, ever see him like that, ever.

Even if it meant him marrying my school librarian.

I had a sudden thought. What if the reason the clasp hadn't appeared for me all through these many Fridays was because Ms. Brock had said *no* to Dad's proposal? What if the key to getting out of this time loop *was* to have the perfect day—but what if I had been completely wrong about what made things perfect?

I stumbled, whacked my elbow into the counter, and knocked my smoothie glass. A big glop of smoothie fell through the air and landed . . .

. . . right on my white sneakers.

"Oh no!" said Dad, grabbing a towel.

"Wait!" I stopped him. "Don't clean it up."

Dad's eyebrows shot up. *"Don't?"*

I swallowed as I let the peach juice soak into the white leather.

"Dad, today is going to be different. And I mean different from any other Friday that has ever come before. Come on. I have a field trip to get to."

On the bus, I watched Ms. Brock. Yup, she was looking preoccupied again, like she had the previous day. Dad had said that they were in love, and I believed him. So why had she said no? I had to figure out what she was thinking and why she rejected his proposal.

"Olive, I have to talk to you," I said as soon as my best friend sat down.

"Is it about the science fair project?" she asked. "Because I'm a little worried that—"

"That 'Texas in the Triassic' is too close to what we did last year. You're totally right, and we should do your idea instead."

"Wait, you do? Because I was kind of thinking we could do the Science of Spying—"

"I love it! Yes, it's way better than my idea. But I'm sorry, I shouldn't have interrupted you just now."

"Oh, it's okay," she said, flustered. "So you're good with

the Science of Spying? We could do something on code-breaking and invisible ink?"

"That sounds great," I told Olive, meaning it. "And I think you have great ideas all the time and we should do them more. And . . . I'm sorry for always taking charge of everything and making you do stuff my way. From now on, we switch off doing your ideas and mine. That way we get to do stuff equally."

Olive leaned away like I was contagious. "Are you feeling okay?"

I smiled. "I'm just having a case of the realizations, that's all."

Jordana took out her blueberry yogurt. Ugh with this danged yogurt! If I had to smell Jordana's vomit one more time . . .

Before she could peel back the lid, I tapped her on the shoulder. "Hey, Jordana. Principal Ramirez was looking for you. Something about leading the announcements next week?"

She perked up. "I've been wanting to get picked to lead announcements forever!"

"He's right outside the bus," I told her. "Here, let me hold your yogurt while you go catch him."

Jordana scooted around me and then practically flew down the aisle. I shoved her yogurt into my backpack. When she got back, I looked up at her. "Sorry. Ms. Hoffman confiscated the yogurt. She said no food on the bus."

Jordana's lower lip quivered. "But . . . my yogie. I have it every day . . ."

Gosh, this girl loved her dairy products. Why didn't I think of this sooner? Now I didn't have to even get out the garbage bag.

"What was that about?" whispered Olive.

"Something I should have figured out about fifty Fridays ago."

The bus arrived at the museum, and we all got off.

"So, should we race through the questions?" asked Olive once Ms. Hoffman started handing out the scavenger hunt sheets.

"Actually, I was thinking that maybe we don't need to win all the points."

Olive did a double take. "Okay, now I know that someone has taken over your body."

"That happened to Addie, not me."

"Who?"

I pulled her to the side. "I kind of need to spend this field trip doing some spying. And I'm going to need your help."

"Spying! You know that's my thing! But this means we won't get enough points and Gabe and Martin are going to win the extra credit."

I took a deep breath and nodded. It was hard to accept. "I know. But I really need to figure something out. This is super important. So can you help me?"

"Are you kidding? I was born for this!"

Once the scavenger hunt started, kids hurried around the museum trying to get the answers. Instead of trying to answer the questions, Olive and I trailed Ms. Brock as she wandered through the exhibits.

Every now and then she'd remind kids to use their walking feet and indoor voices (okay, I guess she didn't just say that to me). But for the most part, she seemed to be really absorbed in checking stuff out.

Olive and I hid around the corner while Ms. Brock went into the *Texas Under the Sea* exhibit. Olive peeked around the edge of the wall so she could see her.

"Can you spot her?" I whispered.

"Tell me again why you want to spy on Ms. Brock?" Olive whispered back.

I sighed. "It's the longest, most complicated story ever. Can you see what she's doing?"

"She's reading the exhibit labels," Olive whispered back. "Oooh, that's kind of interesting . . ."

"What? What's interesting?"

"She's closing her eyes and breathing deeply. She seems really into this one."

"Ready for part two?" I asked Olive. "We're going to be double agents."

"Ready if you are."

Olive and I walked up to the exhibit Ms. Brock was

looking at, pretending to search for an answer to our scavenger hunt questions.

"Oh, hi, Ms. Brock," I said casually. "Are you looking at something in particular?"

"Did you know that millions of years ago, almost all of Texas was covered up by a shallow sea?" she said excitedly. Then she smiled, blushing. "But of course you knew that, Lucy. Your dad says you know this museum inside and out."

"Inside, out, and underneath," I said. "When I was little, I had to come to work with Dad. He used to let me make a fort right there, underneath the *Plesiosaurus* rib cage."

"I think it's very cool that you grew up in this museum," Ms. Brock said. "What a great place to spend your childhood. My parents ran a German restaurant and I had to go with them to work all the time. I could tell you everything there is to know about schnitzel, but that's not quite as cool as the Cretaceous period."

Olive and I laughed. "Ms. Brock, why do you like this exhibit so much?" Olive asked.

She gazed up at the mural that showed Texas covered by crystal-blue water. Blue light rippled over her face. "I always wanted to live by the ocean. Knowing that the sea used to come all the way up here makes me feel like I sort of got my wish. Oh!" She looked down at our paper and then glanced over her shoulder. "You need to leave this hall. I probably shouldn't be telling you this," she whispered. "But the first answer isn't in here. Think about a giant. Hurry, and you might make it!"

Oh my gosh. That very first Friday, I had thought that Ms. Brock was shooing me out of the exhibit. But she was trying to give us a hint!

Olive and I nodded and pretended to be in a rush to get through the questions. As we jogged toward the Hall of Texas Giants, Olive said, "So are you going to tell me why we're spying on Ms. Brock?"

"I think my dad is going to propose to her."

Olive gasped. "And you want to sabotage the proposal?"

"No, of course not! Well, okay, yes, I did want that. But I don't think that's the right thing to do anymore. I think my dad actually might . . ."

"Really be in love with her?" said Olive.

"Yes. And even though I was hesitant at first, I might be starting to realize that . . ."

"Ms. Brock is the sweetest, most amazingest person on earth?" said Olive.

I sighed. "Yes. She is. I know. I'm ridiculous for not figuring it out sooner. So we need to spy on her because even though I know she loves my dad, I think she's on the fence about marrying him. I have to figure out why."

Olive got a bright flicker in her eyes. "Leave everything to me."

Maya, it turns out that there are so many things about my best friend that I had no clue about. For one thing, she is stealthy as a cat.

I was in the dino dig, pretending to search for fossils near the exhibit signs while I waited for Olive to get back from doing something she wouldn't tell me about. And then, totally randomly, I felt my shovel hit something.

I dug down deeper, deeper. I got on my hands and knees and used my fingers. By the time I reached the object, I was a sweaty, dirty mess. I pulled the fossil out of the dirt. I couldn't believe it. It was the *Torosaurus* horn! Gabe was going to be so mad and it was going to be so sweet.

I looked up at the sign right over my head. It said *Paleontological Process* in giant letters. Oh my gosh. Ms. Brock had been trying to give me another hint!

Suddenly, Olive came back and plopped something onto my knees.

I gasped. "Olive! Is this . . . a tiny baby monitor?"

"Yes," she whispered. "Aka the single best piece of home spying equipment ever invented. When Mom was getting rid of all my little brother's baby stuff, I stashed it away. I brought it today in my backpack to show you what I had in mind for the science fair. But now we really get to use it! It's like a one-way walkie-talkie. We'll be able to hear what our teachers are saying, but they won't be able to hear us."

Olive told me how she had set up the monitor receiver behind the bench on the other end of the dino dig. The bench where Ms. Hoffman and Ms. Brock were sitting and sipping their water bottles.

When I looked skeptical, Olive explained, "They're best friends, you know. They go paddleboarding every weekend together."

"Whoa, I had no idea." It was so weird to imagine our teachers having actual lives outside of school.

Olive turned on the baby monitor and dialed it to the same channel as the receiver. She handed it to me. "Here, you listen, and I'll keep digging so no one gets suspicious. Keep the volume low."

I turned the volume dial until I could just barely hear our teachers' voices. I crouched down beside Olive and listened. The first voice I heard was Ms. Hoffman's.

". . . the lake this weekend. But it'll be seventy degrees in the morning—brrrrrr! Time to break out the long underwear."

"Uh-huh," said Ms. Brock.

"Karina, did you hear a word I just said?"

"What?" said Ms. Brock. "Oh yes, long underwear. We might need to wear it. Did you hear it's going to be seventy degrees?"

I could hear some rustling, like one of the teachers was shifting their position on the bench. And then the conversation got really quiet, and I had to dial up the volume on the baby monitor.

"... distracted because you're thinking about Daniel, aren't you?" asked Ms. Hoffman.

Daniel—that was my dad! I put the baby monitor right against my ear.

"Yes," said Ms. Brock with a sigh. "Of course. I can't think about anything else."

"I thought things were going well," said Ms. Hoffman.

"They are. I love him. Very much. But I'm pretty sure that he wants to get serious. Very serious."

"How serious? Move-in-together serious? Engagement serious?"

"I think he's going to propose."

"That's fantastic! Isn't it?"

"No. I just can't do it. It's like I told you. It's Lucy."

My heart felt like it stopped for a second. She was going to reject my dad because of me? Because I was too selfish? Too spoiled? Did she hate me or something?

"I know you were worried that other people would think you were giving her special treatment," Ms. Hoffman said. "Is that it?"

"Well, I was worried about that. But actually, now I feel like I've been way too hard on her and she probably hates me. I've been trying to make up for it, but I don't think she sees it. And . . ." The connection crackled for a second, and I shook the monitor and put it more firmly against my ear. "Lucy and her dad have such a close relationship," she continued. "What if my marrying Daniel messes up their life together? What if I join the family and I don't fit? Or what if Lucy and I get close and then things with Daniel don't work out? What if I make a mess of everything? It's too much pressure."

I stared down at the baby monitor, completely stunned.

"Just tell him you need to slow things down," Ms. Hoffman said.

She sighed. "Yes. Exactly that. I'm feeling overwhelmed."

"Why don't you take a break? I can handle the kids for five, and then we'll head toward the Hall of Gems?"

As I watched Ms. Brock leave the courtyard, I felt frantic. I had to get to my dad. I had to tell him to hold off on proposing. If he proposed now, she would say no for sure and he would be heartbroken. Who knew if they could ever patch that up?

I ran to my backpack to hide the baby monitor, but accidentally ended up dumping everything inside on the ground. Ah! There was no time for this! I left the mess where it was and started sprinting toward my dad's office.

"Hey, that's my yogie!" Jordana gasped. She picked up the yogurt and plastic spoon, peeled back the lid, and started scarfing it down.

"Lucy!" Ms. Hoffman called out to me. "Where do you think you're going?"

"Can I please go up to my dad's office real quick?" I asked.

"Lucy, we have talked about this," Ms. Hoffman said. "Just because your dad works here doesn't mean you can abuse that privilege. You'll have to wait to see him like everyone else."

"But—"

"That's final. Now, in a few minutes, we'll go to the Hall of Gems. Oh! I see you uncovered the *Torosaurus* horn! That makes you and Olive tied with Gabe and Martin for first place for today's activities."

Gabe and Martin looked completely crushed and dejected.

But who cared about the stupid points! I had to talk to my dad.

Jordana started to sway and gurgle. "Ugh . . . I don't feel so good . . ."

Seriously? But we weren't even on a moving vehicle! What was wrong with that yogurt?

"Are you okay?" Olive asked Jordana, walking up to her.

Wait. I had an idea. A disgusting, brilliant idea.

I rushed over to Olive. "Listen, if this doesn't work and it's Friday again, you are not going to remember any of this. But I want you to know that playing spy with you has been probably the coolest thing I've ever done. And you're the best friend anyone could have."

"Lucy, you're not making any sense."

Jordana clutched her stomach. "I think I'm going to be sick . . ."

"Olive, stand back!"

I spun to face Jordana just as her precious yogie upchucked all over me. My cute shirt. My shorts. Definitely my shoes. It was so, so much worse than it had ever been before.

"EWWWWWWW!" cried the entire class.

Ms. Hoffman took one look at me, her eyes wide. "I left

my gym clothes on the bus. Lucy, do you think your dad has a change of clothes in his office?"

I nodded, looking pitiful. Not an act.

She sighed. "Well, Olive, you go with her. Get changed and then come right back to the group. Hurry or you'll miss the Hall of Gems demo!"

✳ 15 ✳

A True Gem

O live and I raced up the stairs and down the hall to Dad's office. But when we got there, the door was locked and the light was out.

"Where is he?"

"Dood we dry downdairs?" said Olive, holding her nose and leaning very far away from me and my yogurt vomit stench.

"Huh? Oh. Should we try downstairs. Yes, let's go!"

We hurried down the back stairwell and to the hallway lined with paleontology lab rooms. At the end of the hall, Gabe stood by the boys' bathroom.

"Hey, Loser-thorn," he said with a smirk. "Looking for Daddy? He went in there."

He nodded to the geology storeroom.

I smirked back. "Thanks, Gabey."

"Dad!" I called as Olive and I ran into the storeroom. He must have been picking out the samples for our demonstration. "Dad, I need to talk to you. Are you there?"

The room was empty.

CLICK!

Olive and I spun around. Oh no. We ran to the door and tried to open it, but it was locked. From the outside.

Gabe put his face to the little window in the door. "You can't get credit for the scavenger hunt or the dino dig if you miss the gems demo, so that means *I'll* get all the points for our science fair project!"

"Are you serious?" I shook the door handle with all my might. "Gabe, let us out of here! You can win! I don't even care about the stupid points!"

"Yeah right, Lucy. You think I believe a word of that? You'll always do or say anything to win. Well, not this time."

He walked away.

"Ugh!" Olive rattled the door and banged on it. She and I yelled for help, but it was no good. The paleontologists were all out on a dig this week, so no one was in this hallway.

"Wait," I said. "We can use Ms. Brock's credit card trick! Remember?"

"Huh?"

"I'll teach you later," I said. "I don't have a credit card, but I do have my museum frequent visitor card in my back pocket . . ."

I jiggled it. One. Two. It worked!

Ah! Ms. Brock really was the best.

We bolted out of the storeroom and searched for our class. The whole second floor was quiet and empty. That meant they had to already be on their way to the Hall of Gems.

"Come on, or we're going to miss the proposal!"

"Wait, what?" Olive asked as we rushed through the hallways. "Your dad is proposing *today*?"

"Yes!"

We raced past *Texas in the Cretaceous, the Pleistocene, and the Holocene.* Finally, we rounded the corner and ran into the dark Hall of Gems.

Dad stood in front of Ms. Brock by the demonstration table. The whole class was staring at them. Dad was holding the diamond and Ms. Brock looked down at the floor as she took a step back from him.

Oh no, no, no.

I was too late.

"Wait!" I shouted.

They both looked up at me. "Lucy?" said my dad, surprised.

I ran to them.

"I just want to say that I fully support this! Ms. Brock, I know you don't think I do, but I really, really do. I think you're kind and smart and sweet and you know cool things like that credit card trick, and you also make my dad incredibly happy."

"You think that?" asked Ms. Brock quietly.

"Yes! And yeah, sometimes things will get messy. Nothing is perfect. But you know what? Nothing has to be perfect. Sometimes it's okay to get dirty. To get covered in yogurt and vomit! I know it won't be easy all the time, and we're going to have ups and downs. But we'll figure it out. And I know my dad loves me and that's never going to change. But even a great family like ours has room for more love, right, Dad?"

"Yeah," Dad said with a smile. "That's right, Lulu."

I turned back to Ms. Brock. "So please, please, Ms. Brock. Marry my dad!"

"Wait. *What?*" Ms. Brock did a double take.

"Marry me?" Dad asked, his eyes wide.

"Yes! Say yes to him!"

My dad flushed bright red. "Lucy," he whispered. "I haven't asked her."

Suddenly, I became aware of every single pair of eyeballs in my class staring at me.

Ohhhhh.

Whoops.

Ms. Brock's eyes were welling up. "Lucy, did you really mean all of that?"

I squared my shoulders. "I did. It would make me really happy, and it would make my dad the happiest guy on earth."

She reached out to hug me.

"Oh, don't! I'm covered in puke and dirt!" I said.

"A little puke and dirt will not stop me," she said, and wrapped her arms tightly around me.

"Well . . . then, since I'm here and holding a diamond," my dad said, smiling. He reached up and took Ms. Brock's hand in his. "Karina Brock, would you do everything that my daughter said and marry me?"

Ms. Brock had the biggest smile I've ever seen. "Yes," she said. "Yes, yes, yes!"

Everyone in the gem room cheered.

My dad pulled both of us into his arms, apparently not caring about puke or dirt, either.

And that, Maya, is how I finally—finally—managed to have the perfect day.

* 16 *

The Last One, Finally

fter the field trip, Ms. Brock—ahem, *Karina*—rode back to school with the class and Ms. Hoffman. Dad took me home to change, shower, and have lunch. Then we went out to my favorite ice-cream place, Draum's. Dad let me save my museum punch card for another day and bought us a banana split.

I couldn't stop smiling. Partly because earlier, when Casper saw me covered in vomit, well, he did his thing, and guess who was standing next to him this time? Gabe Hicks. Thank you, universe.

But I was also happy because my dad was the happiest I had ever seen him.

"Today was really special for me," Dad said as we ate the ice cream together.

"For me, too," I told him. "I'm glad everything worked out the way it did."

Eventually. After who knows how many Fridays?

I looked down at my wrist.

Oh oh oh! The bracelet had a clasp! My clasp had finally appeared! Yes! It worked! Which meant . . . the magic was through. Maybe?

"Dad, can you help me with something?"

"Anything, honey."

I showed him my wrist. "Can you undo the clasp?"

"That's a pretty bracelet. Is it new? And what interesting

stones." His brow furrowed. "I can't tell what those are. They don't quite look like any gems I've ever seen before."

He fiddled with the clasp until it clicked. The bracelet slid off.

I felt a rush of air or wind or something. I relaxed back into my seat. The bracelet was cool in my hand.

"Yeah, it's a pretty unique bracelet," I said. "But it's not mine really. I'm sort of borrowing it."

"Thanks again for everything you said today," Dad said to me as we got up to leave Draum's. "I had no idea that you felt that way about Karina. If I had known, I would have asked her to marry me sooner."

"I guess I just needed a little pressure and a lot of time."

He reached over and squeezed my shoulder. I smiled all the way home.

Dad dropped me off at Mom's at five.

The package was already waiting for me on the porch.

I scooped it up and ran inside.

"Hi!" I called out. "I'm home!"

"Hi, sweetie!" called out Mom. "How was the field trip?"

"So amazing! And I have something very big to tell you! Give me just a minute . . ."

I had to tell Addie and Becca about the bracelet first. I raced up to my room, took out my iPad, called Becca and Addie, and waited for their sweet faces to pop up.

"Hi!" I said. "I'm Lucy! I got your bracelet!"

"Oh! No way!" Addie said. "I just sent it!"

"Wow, magic," Becca said. "That's so great. Don't wish for anything yet, 'kay? We will tell you how it works first."

"Too late!" I cheered. "I made my wish and the bracelet is already off."

"Already?" Addie asked. "How is that possible?"

"Well," I laughed. "It all started this morning . . ."

Once I was off the call with Becca and Addie, I told Mom and Ben all about Dad's proposal to Karina.

"Wow, I wasn't expecting that!" Ben said. "I didn't know they were that serious."

"I knew he had fallen hard for her," Mom said. "I think it's a great match."

"Me too," I said.

"Should we call them to say congratulations?" Ben asked.

Dad had taken Karina out for dinner to celebrate, and we FaceTimed them.

After that, I FaceTimed with Olive.

"Today was so much fun, and I am so happy for your dad," she said. "He's lucky to have you."

"I'm lucky to have him," I said. "And you. Thank you for all your help today. You're an awesome spy."

"Best day ever," Olive said. "And I'll see you tomorrow afternoon."

It was after ten when I finally started getting ready for bed. I realized I hadn't heard Eloise rustling outside. Hmm. What was up with that? Where was she?

I went to my front window and looked out. I could see a fancy car parked up the street that wasn't usually there.

Was that Eloise? What was she doing *there*?

I had no idea.

But I wasn't going to ask.

I got into my bed, looked at my calendar, and closed my eyes. The bracelet was off. But had I really broken the cycle of Forever-Fridays? There was only one way to find out.

The next morning, I woke up to a chubby finger jabbing itself into my cheek.

I opened my eyes.

Kaylee was standing beside my bed, poking me. Kyle was sitting on the floor, chewing the corner of my iPad.

Which meant . . .

I looked around.

I saw the clothes I had been wearing to ice cream with Dad. And my formerly white shoes (Mom had only gone slightly ballistic).

Kyle! Kaylee! Formerly white shoes!

I was at Mom's. I'd woken up at Mom's! Which meant it had worked!

It was Saturday!

The magic had stopped! Hurrah!

I grabbed my iPad and texted Becca and Addie.

Me: Good morning!!!! Do you remember me?

Becca: Of course! Hiiiiiii! 😊 🎉 🧸

Addie: It worked! Congrats!

Me: I have never loved a Saturday more!

Becca: So who do you send the bracelet to next? Whose name does it say on the package?

Oh! I hadn't checked the package. It was still on my desk, where I'd left it last night.

My name and address had been replaced with someone else's!

Me: I have to send it to someone named Maya!

Addie: Maya! Fun!

Becca: Are you going to write her a letter too?

Me: I guess?

Becca: You don't have to, but . . . we did it, and that's how we all got to know each another.

Addie: And then Maya can text us when she gets it! And we can add her to this chain.

Me: Good idea! I'll do it right now.

Addie: Amazing!

Becca: Yay!

* * *

So that's when I decided to write this letter, Maya.

But Mom didn't have any empty notebooks, so I texted Dad that I needed to run over to grab one of his. And while I was walking, I saw that fancy car at the end of the street, in the same spot it had been in last night.

The car door opened, and Eloise stepped out.

I tried to play it cool and keep walking, but she stopped me.

"Hello! Excuse me?" She looked at my empty wrist.

"Can I help you?" I asked, trying to keep a blank face.

"Is there any chance you got a package in the mail? With a bracelet? It was supposed to come to me, but I think it was mislabeled."

Ha. Liar. "No, I don't think so," I said.

"Don't you live on this street?" she asked.

"Me? No. I'm just visiting . . . my librarian. Um, Karina."

"Does she have kids?"

I smiled. "Actually, she has a soon-to-be-stepdaughter. But she's not at the house right now."

"Do you know any other kids on the street?"

"I don't. Sorry. But good luck!"

As I walked away, I started to understand what was going on.

On one of the nights I'd talked to Eloise, she'd said she'd looked at the package and saw the street and the city where the bracelet was going. But not the exact address or the person it was going to. And since I had taken the bracelet off yesterday at the ice-cream parlor, before Addie had sent the package and before the magic had technically turned on, Eloise's tracker had never been activated . . .

Which was why I hadn't heard her last night. Because all she knew was that the bracelet was coming to this street. She didn't know to what house. Or what kid.

And now she never will!

Because in about two minutes, as soon as I finish writing this, I'm going to put the bracelet into the package and mail it all to you, Maya.

And then . . . well, I hope you read my story before you make your wish! I hope you call me and Addie and Becca. Or text us. We can't wait to meet you and help with anything you need. Talk soon, I hope.

XOXOXOX

Best wishes,

Lucy

READ ALL ABOUT BECCA'S AND ADDIE'S ADVENTURES IN:

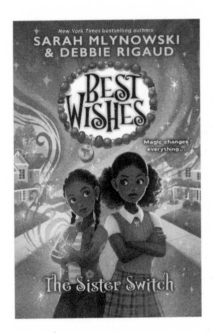

Acknowledgments

We are thankful to all the amazing people who help us time after time after time!

Maxine Vee, who created the gorgeous art and the beautiful cover.

Aimee Friedman, our fabulous editor.

Laura Dail and Stephanie Fretwell-Hill, our brilliant agents.

Thank you to everyone at Scholastic, especially Elizabeth B. Parisi, Melissa Schirmer, Arianna Arroyo, David Levithan, Abby McAden, Ellie Berger, Rachel Feld, Katie Dutton, Erin Berger, Seale Ballenger, Lia Ferrone, Brooke Shearouse, Victoria Velez, Lizette Serrano, Emily Heddleson, Elizabeth Whiting, and everyone in Sales and in the School Channels.

Thanks to Austin Denesuk, Matthew Snyder, and Berni Barta at CAA.

Thanks to the wonderful Lauren Walters, Brittany Schoellkopf, Nicole Caliro, and Stats and the Rosebuds!

Thank you to all our writer friends and family: Tom, Elowyn, Aven, Todd, Chloe, and Anabelle.

Don't miss the *New York Times* bestselling series Whatever After written by Sarah Mlynowski. Fractured fairy tales for fearless kids!

WHAT HAPPENS WHEN YOUR MAGIC GOES UPSIDE-DOWN?

From bestselling authors SARAH MLYNOWSKI, LAUREN MYRACLE, and EMILY JENKINS comes a series about finding your own kind of magic.

DON'T MISS THE BESTSELLING GRAPHIC NOVEL FROM CHRISTINA SOONTORNVAT AND JOANNA CACAO!

"A captivating middle-grade gem."

—*The New York Times Book Review*

★ "Funny, relatable, and genuine."

—*Kirkus Reviews*, starred review

★ "Captures every nuanced emotion."

—*School Library Journal*, starred review

READ THIS CAPTIVATING FANTASY SERIES FROM CHRISTINA SOONTORNVAT!

"With a Thailand-inspired setting, magic rooted in nature and the environment, and whimsical illustrations, this is a promising beginning to a series ready to introduce readers to both the fantasy genre and a beautiful and mysterious new world."

—*Kirkus Reviews*

About the Authors

SARAH MLYNOWSKI is the *New York Times* best-selling author and coauthor of lots of books for tweens and teens, including the Best Wishes series, the Whatever After series, and the Upside-Down Magic series, which was adapted into a movie for the Disney Channel. Born in Montreal, Sarah lived in New York City for many years and now lives in Los Angeles with her family. Visit her online at sarahm.com.

CHRISTINA SOONTORNVAT is the bestselling author of the Newbery Honor books *The Last Mapmaker, A Wish in the Dark,* and *All Thirteen: The Incredible Cave Rescue of the Thai Boys' Soccer Team* and several other books for young readers, including the Legends of Lotus Island series and the graphic novel *The Tryout.* Christina spent a decade working in the science museum field, where she designed programs and exhibits to get kids excited about science and STEM. Christina lives in Austin, Texas, with her husband, two young children, and one old cat. Learn more at soontornvat.com.